"You don't have to stop," Sydney said, pouting

Adam wished he hadn't. His fingers had been almost there, working their way up her thighs, getting closer and closer to home. Then a cupboard had slammed in the kitchen, striking Adam with instant awareness of where he was— and what he'd been about to do. Yanking his hands from Sydney's legs, he rocked back on his heels, his body thrumming, every inch of his flesh aroused. "My sister's in the other room."

"Then let's go somewhere private."

Sydney didn't seem the least bit embarrassed that they'd almost made love, with Adam's sister only a few steps away. Her expression reflected only desire—the hot, unadulterated need to feel his hands on her body, no matter what.

"I don't know you," Adam said.

She learned forward, grabbed his hands and pressed them to her rib cage. Her breathing wasn't quite as steady as she let on, and the moisture seeping through her paper-thin blouse testified to a heat more intense than the ninety-degree temperatures outside. She was burning up from the inside out...and she wanted him to know it.

"You *do* know me, Adam. Better than any man ever has. You just don't remember right now, that's all." She ran her finger over his lips, her voice a throaty purr. "But you will...."

Dear Reader,

Let's clear one thing up right here and now. I am *not* Sydney Colburn. Or rather, she's not me. Yes, she's a romance writer...like I am. Yes, she has a smart mouth...like I do. But that's where the similarities end, I swear. That's the beauty of being a writer—indulging all sorts of fantasies, like wearing designer clothes, driving a candy-apple red Corvette convertible and executing a seduction of a man who looks particularly yummy in blue jeans and a tool belt.

This series—and the book—have been a ball to work on. Not only did I get to revisit several characters from other books (Cassie Michaels from *What's Your Pleasure?* and Jillian Hennessy from *Just Watch Me...*) but I had the chance to work with talented authors Leslie Kelly and Tori Carrington! Our BAD GIRLS CLUB is open to new members, so make sure to stop by my Web site, www.julieleto.com, and sign up!

Enjoy,

Julie Elizabeth Leto

P.S. I've written a BAD GIRLS CLUB novella for the ultimate bad girl, rock-and-roll diva D'Arcy Wilde! Check it out at this month's "Red-Hot Read" at www.eHarlequin.com.

Books by Julie Elizabeth Leto

Julie Elizabeth Leto
BRAZEN & BURNING

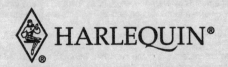

HARLEQUIN®

TORONTO • NEW YORK • LONDON
AMSTERDAM • PARIS • SYDNEY • HAMBURG
STOCKHOLM • ATHENS • TOKYO • MILAN • MADRID
PRAGUE • WARSAW • BUDAPEST • AUCKLAND

For Leslie Kelly, good friend, and Bad Girls Club
head honcho...thanks for inviting me to join this series.
Right up our alleys, huh? When we're bad, we're better.

For Lori & Tony Karayianni, aka Tori Carrington...working with
you never feels like work. Come up and see me sometime.

For Renée Perkie and her generous Ladies Lunch Group...
your support means the world to me. Here's to more good
books, good food and good fun...though on second thought,
goodness has nothing to do with it.

ISBN 0-373-69120-3

BRAZEN & BURNING

Copyright © 2003 by Julie Leto Klapka.

Visit us at www.eHarlequin.com

Printed in U.S.A.

1

To stop the infernal knocking, Sydney Colburn swung her front door open. Bright light sent her stumbling backward, but she managed to catch the doorknob for balance. Unable to form a curse harsh enough to express her ire, she opted to growl.

The person who had driven her to this indignity had the audacity to sound amused. "Are you always this cheery at twelve noon or are you just really happy to see me?"

Sydney squinted, fighting the blinding light—the noon hour explained the glare—to find out who had the frickin' nerve to show up at her door sounding so incredibly buoyant when Sydney had a raging hangover. Her anger deflated when she met Cassie Michaels's eyes—sapphire-blue and wide with nineteen-year-old innocence.

Sydney knew Cassie's innocent act wasn't entirely fake. With a petite body and naturally dark hair plaited in youthful braids that reminded Sydney of Gilligan's Mary Ann, Cassie played the ingenue card for all it was worth. But Sydney had known Cassie too long to completely buy her sweet young thing act. Still, she let her inside the condo anyway. Cassie was, after all, the niece of Sydney's very best friend in the world. The very best friend who was indirectly responsible for her drinking binge the night before. And Syd was pretty sure that Cassie had been the one to make sure she got home safely last night.

"Shut the door before I show you how thrilled I really am," Sydney threatened feebly, stumbling away from the threshold and cursing herself for mixing vodka and rum. Or was it tequila and gin? She didn't remember. She didn't need to remember. Whatever she'd drank the night before had been blended with something pink. Grenadine? Cranberry juice? When she opened her fridge searching for something to quench her thirst and caught sight of a jug of Ocean Spray, she gagged, thankful she had no breakfast in her stomach and, therefore, none on her floor.

Why hadn't she eaten yet if it was noon? Oh, yeah. She'd just woken up. Why had she gotten out of bed again? Right. Loud knocking. Cassie.

The pint-size brunette strolled into her kitchen as if she'd been there a thousand times before. Which she probably had. "Have a good time last night?"

Sydney would have growled again, but she hated to be redundant. "Why are you here?" she asked instead.

"Aunt Devon wanted me to check on you."

"Liar. Devon's on her honeymoon."

Cassie slid a chair out from under the kitchen table, filling Sydney's head with a horrible screeching noise that obliterated the first couple of words of Cassie's answer.

"...drank more than all the groomsmen put together. And I'm a little concerned that binge drinking may be your way of dealing with being the last single woman in your circle of friends."

"Let me guess," Sydney said, pulling out her own chair much more quietly, "the first class you're taking at Tulane is Pop Psychology." She had no intention of answering Cassie's intrusive question. Besides, she didn't have an answer. She didn't want to accept that she'd drunk herself into oblivion last night all on account of a cliché.

Poor, unmarried me. No single friends left to hang with. No man in my life to make my world complete.

Blech.

"No, but I read Dr. Phil's newest book on my plane ride home for the wedding," Cassie answered. "Besides, I'm nineteen. That makes me a certifiable expert on everything, remember?"

Remember what? Nineteen? Sydney snorted. She couldn't remember last night, much less something that had occurred over eleven years ago. Besides, she'd tried damned hard to suppress most memories from around ages ten to twenty. Those years were formative and filled with more mistakes, missteps and misery than she ever wanted to relive.

However, just around the time of her twenty-first birthday, Sydney had made a decision to buck the system of her New England upbringing and live without apologies. She did what she wanted, when she wanted. She spoke the truth, even when people didn't want to listen. She played the stock market like a blackjack table—and won. She wrote widely popular, highly subversive historical romance novels where the women were strong and smart and could bring hulking knights and bloodthirsty warriors to their knees.

And whenever she could, she took lovers the way

most men did—with emphasis on immediate physical payoff and avoiding commitment. For the past decade, Sydney's carefree, unrepentant lifestyle had worked wonders. She'd graduated from college, made a successful career for herself as a novelist and collected a small but loyal group of friends who accepted her for who she really was. Not to mention that she had a love life that would make even the most sexually satisfied heroines in her books pea-green with envy.

And, yes, last night she'd become the last single woman in that loyal group of friends, excluding Cassie, who was too young to really count, though rumor had it her innocent young friend had recently met a college boy and was, officially, smitten. Who knew how long it would be before Sydney was throwing a wedding shower for a bride thirteen years her junior?

Oh, well. She'd throw one hell of a party. Sydney'd never planned to get married anyway. She hadn't drank too much last night because she'd felt lonely or left out or any other weepy sentiment on the dark side of the emotional spectrum.

She'd drank too much last night because drinking too much was the only thing she could think to do since her life suddenly came to a stop. And not because of Devon's wedding. She was genuinely happy for Devon. As Cassie's legal guardian, Devon Michaels had spent most of her adult life caring for her niece at the expense of her own personal fulfillment. Sydney had toasted her friend and fellow writer with great gusto and premium poetic words. She liked to think she had a hand in the romance of her mystery novelist friend and Jake Tanner, the hunky former cop Devon had married. She'd encouraged their relationship from the start and had no regrets.

No, Sydney Colburn's life had come to a stop at precisely five o'clock Wednesday afternoon—a full three days prior to the wedding—simply because she'd reached the pinnacle of her career. Her newest book, a hardcover historical set on the moors of Scotland, had debuted in the number one spot on the coveted *New York Times* bestseller list. She'd achieved her single most important dream, as evidenced by the newspaper Cassie had carried into the condo and was now spreading carefully over Sydney's butcher-block tabletop.

"Congratulations. I hear you kicked some literary ass last week," Cassie said, attempting to couch her understated tone with a wry grin.

"Apparently," Sydney grumbled.

Sydney had dreamed about this day since she first learned there ever was such a thing as a bestseller list. These novels were in such demand by booksellers and readers across the country that the titles and authors' names were printed in the country's most prestigious newspaper.

"Aunt Dev said you've wanted this all your life."

"Well, I don't think I wanted it when I was four," Sydney quipped. "My main ambition then would have been a Malibu Barbie with a cool Corvette convertible."

"You drive a Corvette convertible," Cassie pointed out. "There may be a connection."

Sydney raised her eyebrows, wincing as the simple movement made her head throb all the more. "You think?"

Cassie sighed in the way only someone younger than twenty could. Sydney glanced at the refrigerator again, wondering if that "hair of the dog that bit you" saying was true. She owned at least one bottle of vodka or gin or rum or tequila. She vaguely remembered a fully stocked wet bar somewhere in the living room. She didn't drink much, but when she did, she made it count. Only, she didn't really want more alcohol. She wanted to get rid of the kid, so she could go back to wallowing in peace.

"When you set a goal, you set a goal," Cassie continued, obviously intent on having this deep psychological conversation even if Sydney didn't want to. Oh, well. Why fight it? She didn't have anyone else to hash this out with.

Devon was on her honeymoon, and while the others in her circle were good for shopping excursions and beachside lunches, none of them were writers. They supported her career by buying her books and talking them up to anyone willing to listen to their pitch, but none of them would really understand the downside of her reaching her ultimate goal. Even though they knew her profession held little of the glamor the media hyped and they respected her hard work, they could see no negatives to her job. She made up stories for a living. She'd just reached a major accomplishment in popular fiction—her name above Clancy, Grisham and Roberts, for this week at least. So while she'd tried to talk to them about how lost she felt, they couldn't get beyond excited congratulations.

She loved them for the support—she really did. But

support or not, she still felt like a drifting boat on a wind-tossed sea.

She wasn't even sure that Cassie, who'd grown up in Devon's care and knew more about the publishing business than most literary agents, would truly understand. How could she when Sydney didn't? She'd accomplished her dream years before she expected to, and still she wasn't happy. Why wasn't she flying off to New York to celebrate with her editor? Why wasn't she searching out a ladder so she could shout her accomplishment from the top of her three-story condominium building?

God, her head hurt.

"I don't want to talk about this, Cassie."

"You sound like my mother."

Sydney's shoulders drooped. "Did you come here to help or to insult me?"

Cassie's mother was the Grammy-award-winning rock 'n' roll phenomenon, D'Arcy Wilde. Of all the sexy acts out there giving music lovers their MTV, only Darcy could make Madonna look like June Cleaver in a push-up bra. Madonna at least raised her own children. Darcy had pawned Cassie off on her sister Devon, and she continued to lead a wild life, trotting from one gig to the next, building a personal empire on a foundation of provocative videos and sold-out concert tours. Though Sydney and Darcy had been compared to each other many times because of their open attitudes toward sex and men, neither of them took the association as a compliment.

In short, they despised one another.

"You know, my mother likes you," Cassie claimed.

"She also likes tearing strategic holes in her T-shirts and playing peek-a-boo with her nipples on stage. I should be flattered?"

Cassie laughed. "Darcy likes to shock people. So do you."

"That's where you're wrong. In order to like shocking people, you actually have to care about what people think about you. I don't give a damn."

Clearing her throat, Cassie nodded. "But you gave a damn about making the *Times* list. So what's next?"

"Sex on the beach," Sydney concluded.

"Oh, yeah. Drinking more is the solution."

"I wasn't talking about the drink. I'm going to the beach to pick up some glistening hunk, and then I'm going to have sex."

It had been a long time since Sydney had indulged in an anonymous affair. Too long. She searched her mind for a face—names were usually optional—and she couldn't place one. Hmm. In fact, the first face that came to mind—rugged, handsome and highlighted by the most unusual almond-tinted eyes she'd ever seen—belonged to Adam Brody. God. Adam Brody. He'd literally disappeared out of her life over a year ago, though he still he managed to creep into her thoughts every so often. At weak moments.

"I shouldn't be telling you about my love life," Sydney said.

"You're not ashamed of your free-love lifestyle, are you?" Cassie asked, her tone a tad too suspicious for Sydney's liking.

"The fact that Sydney and shame start with the same letter is the only connection between me and that emotion," she assured her. "On the other hand, I don't want to corrupt you. My lifestyle is just that—*my* lifestyle. My choices aren't for everyone."

"Ain't that the truth," Cassie concluded. She scraped her chair back and headed toward the fridge, which Sydney noticed she'd left open.

As she watched Cassie rise on her tippy-toes to peer behind the carton of week-old skim milk, Sydney realized something.

The kid was wearing makeup.

In all the years she'd known her, from way back when Cassie's main concern in life revolved around Beanie Babies, throughout childhood and her teen years, Cassie chose her clothes for comfort and brushed her hair only after her aunt threatened to withhold her allowance. She eschewed high school homecoming dances and proms in favor of opera night or a hockey game. So why did the levelheaded, giggle-free Cassie suddenly look like an ideal candidate for *Temptation Island*?

That rumor she'd heard about Cassie and a boy-friend must have been true. No wonder she was suddenly so concerned with the state of Sydney's life. No one could be more meddling than a young woman in love.

Cassie retrieved a jug of orange juice and shut the door. "You can have your choices, Sydney. Thanks to you and my mother, I have lived a vicarious wild life I won't ever need to experience for myself."

Sydney raised an eyebrow, watching through bleary eyes as Cassie retrieved two glasses, filled them, and replaced the jug. She'd always known the kid was ma-

ture beyond her years and had had amazing insights
since she was old enough to speak in sentences, but
sometimes she still surprised Sydney. Mainly because
Sydney constantly underestimated her young friend.

"You're sure?" Sydney asked. "Most kids your age
are just clamoring to live life on the edge."

Cassie visibly shivered. "Most kids today aren't
raised on the edge."

"Devon made sure your life was normal," Syd reminded her.

"Thank God. But I eavesdropped on your little tête-
à-têtes with my aunt during Tuesday-night poker. And
I watched *Entertainment Tonight* at least once a week to
find out which boy toy my mother had most recently
dumped."

Cassie placed one OJ in front of Sydney, then shook
out two aspirin from the bottle she found in the cabinet
over the sink. Sydney downed them greedily.

"It's safe to say I'm immune from wanting to be like
you or my mother," Cassie concluded.

Sydney sighed in relief, pressing her hand to her
throbbing brow. "I'm glad to hear it."

Cassie slid back into the chair across from hers. "You
look horrible—you know that, right?"

"Doesn't come as a big surprise."

"Picking up some nameless hunk might not be an
easy feat."

Sydney chuckled. "Maybe that wasn't the best idea
I've had."

Cassie leaned back, then kicked her feet onto the
chair beside hers. "Mom bought me a spa package over

at Safety Harbor for graduation that I still haven't used. I'd bet they'd fit us in on short notice—you being a *New York Times* bestselling author and all."

"Oh, and the fact that your mother is D'Arcy Wilde would have nothing to do with it?"

"Couldn't hurt..."

The idea sounded tempting, even to Sydney in her foggy condition. But after spending the day being salted, exfoliated, massaged and pampered, what then? She'd still have the same problem that she'd had for the past four days. She had no idea what she was going to do next with her life or career.

She'd made the *New York Times* list before, and had reaped the benefits. Her bulldog of an agent had manipulated her repeated appearances in the top fifteen of the bestseller list into a multimillion dollar contract—a contract Sydney had just fulfilled by turning in the last book. Making the list the first few times had been a rush—so much so that she had set debuting at number one as a goal to work toward for the rest of her career.

Who'd have known she'd succeed so quickly?

She felt like a fraud. A directionless, ungrateful fraud.

"I have no right to feel depressed, you know," Sydney admitted.

"If the constitution had been written by the Founding Mothers rather than the Fathers, the right to be depressed in the face of good fortune would have been second on the list."

Sydney grinned, even though the action made her cheeks ache. "I should be shouting from the rooftops!

Please tell me I'm insane. I'd hate to think a sane person would feel so lost when they'd just achieved the one thing they wanted more than anything in the world."

"Maybe if you had someone to share your victory with..."

"I've shared, sweetheart. With Devon—"

"—who was mostly too wrapped up in her wedding to really celebrate with you."

"I called my mother."

"And?"

"She called all her friends at the country club. They want me to speak to their ladies' lunch group next month."

"You haven't spoken to them before?"

"They kept telling me I couldn't mention sex."

"Now you can?"

"I debuted at number one on the *New York Times.* I could talk about belching and farting in the fifteenth century and they'd think I was just charming. Oh, God. Please don't tell me I just earned the right to be eccentric."

"You've been eccentric since I met you. But when you're under sixty-five, it's called something else."

"Don't tell me what."

"I wasn't going to."

"Value your life, do you?"

"As much as you value your Barbie Corvette."

"Okay, so I shared with the people I care about most. So now what?"

"Pick a new goal?"

Sydney shook her head. What else was there? She already had the best job in the entire world. She spent long hours every day in her fantasy world, making up stories about hot sex and deep love, and someone paid her money to do it. Not that she needed the money. With her handy-dandy trust fund, she would have been set for life if she'd never typed a word. But when she'd received the first third of her legacy at eighteen, she'd started her foray into the world of stocks and investments. By the time she'd received the second third, not only was she earning a living as a writer, but she'd also doubled the investments she'd made the first time around. Sydney learned she had a head for three things—history, sex and money.

And as a successful historical romance novelist, she'd worked those strengths into a damned great career. She even enjoyed an ideal celebrity status, appearing at crowded book signings and on television and radio interviews, yet she could still go to the grocery store or the mall without being accosted.

To top it all, she served on the board of a foundation that provided literacy training in poor neighborhoods. Hell, she volunteered her time twice a month.

"What's left, Cassie? God! I must be the most shallow woman on earth to have accomplished everything she wanted to do by the time she was thirty-two."

Cassie shook her head. "Not shallow. Not really."

Sydney cocked her eyebrow. She'd heard a "but" in there somewhere.

"What do you mean, 'not really'?"

Anyone with more sense would have shrugged and begged off pointing out Sydney's shortcomings, but Cassie, in her youthful confidence and ignorance, settled into her chair. "On the surface, you have an ideal life. Money, friends, a great career."

"The foundation. Don't forget the foundation."

Cassie grinned. "Yes, you even do charitable work. You've been very careful and calculating, organizing your life with precision."

"Hey, let's not get insulting. I don't organize. I fly by the seat of my pants."

At this, Cassie frowned. "You like to think so."

"Think so? I'm famous for my haphazardness. Ask your aunt. She rags me all the time for being such a mess."

"That's because Aunt Devon has elevated organization and planning to a religion. Compared to her, you are a mess. But compared to the normal population of the world, you've mapped out your entire life, ending with debuting your novel at number one on the *New York Times* bestseller list. Am I right here?"

Sydney couldn't argue, not only because of her pounding headache, but because the kid made sense.

"But you don't have someone to love."

With a groan, Sydney folded her arms on the table and laid her forehead down. Gently. This verified her earlier suspicion. Young Cassie was in love and wanted to share her joy.

Great. Just great.

"God, please save me from being the clichéd heroine of a romance novel!" Sydney wailed dramatically before skewering her inexperienced friend with a powerful glare. "You know, that line in *Jerry Maguire* was written by a man. I do not—I repeat—I do *not* need a man to complete me. If you really subscribe to such thinking, you've set feminism back to the days of Susan B. Anthony."

Sydney managed to keep her head lifted long enough to watch Cassie laugh, but she didn't see the humor. This wasn't funny.

"Call it the new feminism. I'm not saying you need a man to complete you. But you could use a shot of something deeper, don't you think? An emotional experience to challenge you and your status quo. *Someone* to challenge you and your status quo."

Ah, so this mystery boy had shaken up Cassie's life. Bully for her. Sydney was long past such a beginning-of-life discovery.

"No such man exists," Sydney concluded.

"Have you looked?"

No.

"Of course I have."

"And no guy ever rocked your world a little, shook you up so badly you had to walk away or risk losing your heart?"

Damned if Adam Brody's rugged face didn't pop right back into Sydney's brain again, causing an electric charge to spark low in her belly and shoot to the tips of her breasts. The man had been an incredible lover. Selfish when it suited him, yet giving at the core. So incredible, in fact, that while with him, Sydney had broken so many of her self-imposed dating rules that she'd done more than risk her heart—she'd risked her very soul.

Yet, when he'd asked her to make their affair about commitment and love rather than just sex, she'd walked away. Actually, ran was more like it. Scared and out of her element, like a second grader enrolled in high school calculus. Sydney had mustered her cool enough to exit with style, but she still couldn't get the man off her mind. Not on the eight-hour flight to London the day after she'd left him, not through the month-long tour through Scotland, or the seemingly endless three weeks in New England with her parents. When she'd finally returned and had decided to give in and take a chance on his offer, he'd disappeared off the face of the earth.

He'd sold his condo, deactivated his cell phone, closed his business. He'd once told her he was considering relocation to Baltimore to partner with his former mentor, so she'd assumed that's what he'd done. And being a woman who never announced her regrets—rarely even to herself—she'd simply moved along, writing her books, playing poker with Devon on Tuesdays, traveling for autographings and research, and taking a handsome lover whenever her body needed release.

But maybe Cassie was on to something. Maybe she needed a male-female relationship less predictable than one based only on sex. Orgasms she could give to herself. She needed an affair equal to a cache of fireworks—haphazard, chancy—a true risk that might rock her world back into the tumble of chaos she so enjoyed.

And who better to fire her wick than sexy Adam Brody?

"Know any good private investigators?" she asked.

Cassie lurched forward, her young eyes alight with intrigue. "As a matter of fact...you remember Jake's best man? Cade Lawrence? His wife, Jillian, is a P.I. A darned good one from what I hear."

Sydney nodded, sat up straighter and downed her orange juice, finishing the entire tumbler. She tried to comb her fingers through her hair, but a mass of tangles stopped her progress. Oh, yeah. She looked like crap.

That, at least, she could fix.

"Get me her number, then make yourself comfortable. I'll be down in twenty."

"Dare I dream you've taken my advice to heart?"

Sydney grabbed a pad of paper from a drawer beneath her telephone, then tossed it and a pencil at her young friend. "After you write down Jillian's number, call the spa and throw some weight around. I'm in desperate need of a facial."

Cassie's chuckle followed Sydney out of the kitchen and through the living room, toward the staircase to her bedroom. She wondered if Adam would be excited to see her, or was he still angry? He'd been fairly pissed the night she'd walked out of his condo, shamelessly sticking to her rule about not getting emotionally involved with any man. She'd insulted him to the core, just by telling him no. And she hadn't explained. Why should she? She'd been up front with him from the moment they'd banged into each other while jogging around a corner of his building. One bang had led to another, and she'd been clear about the fact that she wanted nothing more than sex and maybe a few laughs from their affair.

Trouble was, they'd had more than that from the get-go. Adam had been intelligent, witty, charming—a fine match for her razor-sharp sarcasm. He was a driven businessman who lost himself in his blueprints and designs just as she went MIA during the best parts of her books. And from the dinner table conversation to the acrobatics in the bedroom, he had never failed to give as good as he got, which was probably why the affair had lasted six months longer than a one-night stand.

Then he'd made the ultimate mistake. The night before she was leaving for a book tour and research trip, he asked her to stay the night with him. It had seemed like such a small request, Sydney remembered, her gaze drawn to the bay window, the one that had once faced his across the courtyard. But his suggestion hadn't been small at all. He'd asked her to break a major rule in her dating constitution...and she'd already bent more rules for him than she had for any other man. He'd even admitted he'd intended to entice her to spend the night as his first step in luring her to try settling down.

Sydney bristled, more out of habit than true discomfort over the idea of hearth and home. She wasn't a fool—she understood and accepted the awesome power of a committed relationship. She wrote romance novels, for Pete's sake. She usually even teared up when she penned the happy ending. But she also knew that true love relationships came at the price of compromise and change, perhaps even a complete overhaul of life choices and personal goals. The kind of overhaul she might be ready for now, but hadn't been when Adam had asked.

So she'd walked. Just as she was walking now with the same purposeful, unapologetic stride, ending up in the same place, in the hall outside her bedroom—alone.

On the wall next to the thermostat hung her most cherished collectible—a framed movie poster from the classic 1933 film *She Done Him Wrong*, starring Mae West. Sydney had admired the woman since the first time she'd stayed home sick from her exclusive Boston private school and watched a marathon of the actress's old movies on television. Irreverent, powerful, sexy Mae had inspired Sydney on varying levels throughout her life. By the time she was twenty, Sydney had turned a flash of cinematic curiosity into a full-fledged motion-picture obsession. The actress's autograph graced the lower left corner of the yellowing cardboard, but it was the quote across the top that Sydney treasured most.

She read the snippet aloud, injecting herself with the confidence she'd need to not only find Adam Brody, but to entice him back into her bed—and into her life.

"Listen," she read, not bothering to try to mimic Mae's distinctive voice when she knew she couldn't, "when women go wrong, men go right after them."

Sydney raised her nightshirt over her head as she headed toward her shower, reveling in the cool blast of air tingling over her suddenly heated skin. "I hope you're right, Mae. I sure as hell hope you're right."

2

ADAM BRODY STRETCHED his arms over his head, working the kinks out of the muscles in his shoulders. He twisted his neck side to side, comforted by the resounding snap, crackle and pop. Damn, it felt good to move like this. Even the tug of the long scar that stretched from his lower back to his skull didn't stab like a razor anymore. Only mild discomfort. A small price to pay.

After one last glance at the raging noon sun sizzling his skin wherever the rays broke through the canopy of camphor trees and water oaks, Adam returned his attention to the plans laid out on his ramshackle workbench—an old back door balanced on wooden sawhorses. He grabbed a nail and his hammer, then squinted at the pencil drawings, concentrating on the next step in his creation. He did his best to ignore the anger that surged whenever he had to use the majority of his brain power do something so basic as mark the next step in building a child's custom playhouse.

"Adam!"

His sister's call from the back porch effectively destroyed his tenuous concentration. He looked up, fighting his annoyance for one reason only. If not for Renée, he wouldn't be here, working in the sun, making himself useful. He'd probably still be in rehab, fighting his physical therapists and doctors, raging against the broken bones and ripped muscles that refused to obey his commands. He owed her so much.

So why did he still harbor resentment?

He had no idea, and his brain still hurt too much to work it out.

"Yeah?" he answered.

"Someone just came through the front gate. Do you see a car?" Renée lifted her hands, caked with something white. Could be either flour or paint, but whatever it was, she didn't want any visitors seeing her in such a mess.

Adam grinned. *Women.*

He walked a few paces to the side of the old log cabin his father had built with his own hands forty years ago and had left to them both after his death. Before Adam's accident, Renée had used the property during the weekdays, mainly for her business, while he had commandeered the place on weekends for fishing excursions with his buddies. After the accident, Renée had insisted they both live there full-time, certain the serene setting would aid his recovery. Off the beaten path in a still-undeveloped section of Florida's Hernando County, Adam and Renée didn't receive many unexpected visitors. The occasional developer came by, looking to purchase the thirty acres they owned on Lake Simpson, fed by the tributaries of Homosassa Springs. A fisherman might wander in, looking for a place to lower his johnboat into the water and catch some large-mouthed bass. A stray tourist occasionally got lost on the winding dirt roads that led to this untouched paradise.

But this visitor looked completely out of place. Developers knew to drive a truck or four-wheel-drive vehicle when maneuvering through the spongy terrain in this part of the wilderness. And while tourists might make an error in judgment by taking their minivans and station wagons off the paved roads, no fisherman he knew pulled a johnboat with a shiny, candy-apple-red Corvette convertible.

And no fisherman he knew had long flaming red hair that caught the sunlight and reflected back copper fire. When the driver, distinctly female, stopped in front of the cabin, a swirling cloud of dry Florida dirt shielded his view of her. Adam dropped his hammer on the workbench and grabbed the dark blue bandanna he'd shoved into his back pocket.

By the time he'd marched to the front of the house, the dust had settled. The driver checked her face in the vanity mirror, though why, Adam had no clue. Even from twenty feet, he could tell she was perfect. Creamy skin. Glossy red lips. Dangling gold earrings that, like her auburn hair, captured and reflected the light from the sun. This woman was beautiful—and totally out of her element in the Florida boonies.

When she spotted him, she grinned. Adam stopped. Did she know him? The smile was too small to tell. He immediately glanced down at his shirtless chest and low-slung jeans. The woman's expression might have been subtle, but he recognized predatory when he saw it.

She got out of the car and walked around the front end wearing a slim pair of white-washed jeans, a tiny, ribbed tank top beneath a fluttery, sheer blouse and death-defying high-heeled sandals. No doubt the look of the hunter now darkened his face, as well.

Grrrr.

"Can I help you?" he asked.

"Well, that depends," the woman said. She leaned against the hood of her car just over the right front wheel, her hips moving just enough to draw his attention to the gentle flare of her lower body, encased in denim, but begging for the exploration of his hands. Her eyes, green as the pine trees swaying in the gentle lake breeze, grabbed the fire from her hair and sparked her irises with intentions he couldn't yet read. But he knew she was up to no good. This woman had *bad girl* written all over her. And by the tilt of her grin, she knew it.

He wiped the sweat off his palms. "You lost?"

A flash of confusion, clear from a quick downturn of her lips, dimmed her potent sensuality, but only momentarily. Whatever she thought she didn't understand, she obviously decided to ignore it. "No, actually, I'm found. Well, you're found. You aren't an easy man to track down, you know."

A string of curses shot through Adam's brain, but he'd at least learned to keep the frustration contained. She knew him, likely from his former life in Tampa, but he didn't know her. The situation happened less and less often now that he'd accepted that his old life didn't fit him so well anymore.

Out here near Homosassa Springs, he had a few visitors from time to time, mainly friends and neighbors he'd known since childhood. They were people whose relationship with him had hardly been touched by the accident, who could hang out for an entire afternoon playing football without mentioning the tragedy one single time. People he trusted.

And even in the ninety-degree afternoon sun, this woman looked cool as ice. Sure, a little perspiration moistened her skin from her upper lip to the concave of flesh between her breasts, but everything else about her shouted "cool operator."

Any minute now, he expected a protective barrier to rise around him, to provide quick immunity to the woman's undeniable appeal. He waited, but no such wall emerged. Maybe he was done gating himself off from the unknown. Maybe he'd become more his old self than he had wanted to see before today.

She smiled.

He smiled back.

"I didn't know anyone was looking for me," he said.

She bounced off the hood and closed the distance between them in several long, purposeful strides. She wasn't tall by any means—the top of her head barely reached his chin—but her slender build and go-get-'em attitude nearly made him take a step back.

Nearly, but not quite.

When she slid her fingertips over the ridge of his collarbone, he nearly bolted out of his skin.

Nearly, but not quite.

Holding still while she stroked his flesh proved tougher than some of the exercises he'd done in rehab. A new layer of perspiration coated his skin. And a certain part of his anatomy didn't cooperate in his quest to remain unaffected by her bold, exploratory touch. He glanced down, hoping his loose jeans would keep that telltale sign of his attraction from her view.

When he looked up, he watched her brazenly retrace the path of his gaze. His hardness sparked a flare in her smile.

"Oh, so you *are* happy to see me. I shouldn't have taken so long to track you down."

He could tell she was trying to hide the regret in her voice with her loaded innuendo and her naughty glimpse of his crotch. She might have succeeded if it hadn't been for the intense seriousness in her green eyes.

"This isn't one of those 'where have you been all my life?' moments is it, lady? Because, luscious as you are, I have work to do."

"Lady?" Her surprise rang clear. "Don't play with me, Adam. I know I pissed you off last time I saw you, but what's done is done. And I've come a long way to tell you I was wrong. Can't you forgive and forget?"

She allowed her hand to lazily drop down his chest, her fingers burrowing a path through the layer of sweat and dirt on his skin, ending when she pulled her hand away at his navel.

"I already forgot, I'm afraid," he answered. "Whether I wanted to or not."

She bit her bottom lip, tugging the bright red flesh between straight white teeth. "Good. That'll make everything easier."

Adam opened his mouth to tell her otherwise when he heard the front door of the cabin swing open, then bang shut.

"Adam?"

He turned in time to see Renée take one step down off the rough steps. She twisted a towel around her hands, wiping clean whatever white paint or powder she'd been working with before. She'd run a brush through her straight blond hair, undoing the ponytail she wore each and every day. She'd tucked in her T-shirt. Put on shoes. All cleaned up, she looked more like the barely twenty-one-year-old coed she'd been before their parents' deaths robbed her of most of her youthful exuberance. Before his accident swiped the rest.

Adam didn't know why, but his sister's sudden attention to her appearance in the presence of this stranger put him on edge.

"Everything all right?" she asked.

The woman from the convertible frowned deeply, then arched a brow. "Tell me she's your sister." More a command than a request, her voice remained low so that Renée couldn't hear.

Adam obliged. "She *is* my sister."

The stranger blew out a low whistle. "Thank God."

She put on her best smile and sashayed across the yard, managing to look graceful and surefooted as her four-inch heels bit into the grass and mulch.

The woman had sass. He couldn't be sure if this had been a trait he'd found attractive before, but he sure as hell found it hot now.

"You must be Adam's sister. I wish I could say he told me a lot about you, but that wouldn't be true."

She extended her hand to Renée, but his sister responded by throwing a perplexed look his way. After a moment, the stranger turned and hit him with the same expression.

She mouthed the word *Well?*

He shrugged.

"No manners, huh?" the stranger said. "Men."

She looked to Renée for some indication that she commiserated, but his sister looked far too uncomfortable to do more than stand there. Renée didn't like situations she didn't understand and, therefore, couldn't control. He'd been told he'd once been the same way, but lately "live and let live" made for a much less frustrating lifestyle.

Suddenly, he realized what the stranger wanted—she wanted him to introduce her to his sister. Well, he couldn't, could he? So he shrugged again, then strolled closer, positioning himself between the two of them, though he wasn't exactly sure why. He hooked his thumbs in the leather of his tool belt and trusted his instincts. Lately, they were all he had.

The stranger rolled her eyes, then extended her hand to his sister again. "I'm Sydney Colburn."

Renée glanced at him with a thousand questions she knew as well as he did that he couldn't answer. Finally, she accepted the handshake. "Renée Brody. Wait. Sydney Colburn, the romance novelist?"

"You know my books?"

Surprisingly, the sexy stranger did humility very well.

"There's not much to do out here after dark," Renée answered, and Adam wasn't sure if his sister had just extended the woman a compliment or not. He sighed. Sometimes, Renée was better off living in the woods—

her interpersonal skills sucked. Then again, her blunt style had helped him get the best medical care her sharp tongue could buy. "I read quite a bit," she continued, her tone quick, as if she meant to undo the damage. "You know my brother?"

Sydney eyed her narrowly. "Biblically."

Adam coughed, stunned by the woman's brazen statement, which she punctuated with an unabashed wink.

Renée obviously didn't believe her. "I don't see how that can be possible. Adam would have told—"

"Oh, I doubt Adam would have told you anything about me. It wasn't the way we worked. Back then."

When the mysterious, sexy Sydney Colburn slid her hand up his bare arm, Adam watched two things prickle—the hair on his forearm and his sister. If Renée had had hackles, they would have raised to full attention.

Uh-oh. He'd seen her go into protection mode before, and the results could be ugly.

"Adam tells me everything. We're very close."

Sydney seemed undaunted, oblivious to Renée's darkening mood. Her mouth quirked up on one side as she took in her surroundings. "Close, huh? Are we talking close like backwoods kissin' cousins or is my mind just dipping into the gutter again? I swear, I've been trying to fix that about myself but it's a tough-won battle."

Renée's shock knocked all pretense of hospitality off her face. "Who the hell do you think you are?"

"I told you, I'm Sydney Colburn."

She left it at that—as if the mere statement of her

name should be sufficient to fill in all the blanks. Renée crossed her arms over her chest and squared her stance, as if preparing for battle.

And while Adam enjoyed a good catfight the same as any man, he had to step in. He had a strong suspicion that this Sydney Colburn, even in tight jeans and towering sandals, was the one woman who could give his scrappy sister a run for her money.

"Yes, you are Sydney Colburn, and this is Renée Brody. And I am, indeed, Adam Brody, who you apparently came a long way to find. Renée, do you think you could give us a minute?"

Renée's blue eyes flashed and her lips rolled inward to form a grim line of indignation. "I don't know if that's a good idea," she muttered.

Adam glanced down at Sydney, who had the sense to keep her mouth shut, though, for some reason, he suspected she had a razor-sharp quip dancing on the edge of her tongue.

"I'm really thirsty," he insisted. "Could sure use some of your world-famous lemonade."

He quirked his smile with a dash of charm, which softened his sister. Two months ago, he wouldn't have been able to execute such a smooth maneuver. Little by little, he was remastering the art of female manipulation.

Without another word, Renée stomped back into the house. He noticed that while she'd pulled the screen door shut, she'd left the inner door open. His sister had never been known for her subtlety—something else she seemed to have in common with Sydney Colburn, who'd just latched on to his arm.

"I should have been nicer to your sister. But, man, I could sense her antagonism a mile away." She shook her head, and Adam couldn't resist taking a deep breath, inhaling the scent of lavender that floated around her. Soft and soothing, in direct contrast to the brazen woman who wore it—almost. She said what was on her mind, but she also took instant responsibility for her brassiness. "I go on the defensive sometimes before I can stop myself. What did you tell her about me?"

He took her hand, the one that had been making love to his forearm, and dragged her back toward her car. "I didn't tell her a damned thing. I couldn't."

"Well, you *could* have. I mean, I know we had an agreement not to tell anyone about us, but that was a long time ago. You might have talked about me. Once."

They reached the Corvette in time for Adam to figure out that she was miffed by his silence. If she only knew what was really going on...

"Listen, I don't know what you're thinking, but assuming that we once knew each other—"

"Assuming?"

Her eyebrows shot up. When she wrenched her hand free, he had no choice but to let go.

"Adam, I realize I was adamant about keeping our affair quiet and all about sex and nothing about our personal lives, but I got the distinct impression that when I left you, you didn't want me to go."

"*You* left *me?*"

Adam didn't know why, but that fact didn't sit well. Didn't jive with what his sister had told him about his prior affairs and love interests. In Renée's estimation, he'd broken a string of hearts the length of Interstate 75. He'd been so wrapped up in his career as a hotshot, innovative architect that he'd never married, never fallen in love. And though Renée claimed he didn't keep his lovers around for more than a couple of months, she had memorized the complete list of the women he'd told her about.

And the list didn't include anyone named Sydney Colburn, a woman who'd supposedly dumped him.

"You find that hard to believe?" she asked, apparently getting annoyed.

"Surprisingly...yes."

"Sorry, sweetheart, but you broke the rule. You asked me to stay the night with you, and that was...against the rule," she repeated hotly. The flush on her skin darkened from light pink to magenta and she stamped her foot.

God, she was sexy when she lost her temper. Actually, he figured this woman had written the original definition of sexy, from her long, wavy auburn hair to her peek-a-boo blouse and skintight jeans. Suddenly, imagining that they'd once been involved wasn't so hard to believe.

"We had rules?"

"Don't toy with me, Adam. Of course we had rules! We wouldn't even have exchanged last names, except we lived in the same complex and read each other's mailboxes every day. Why am I telling you this? You know. You know me. You know what I'm like...what I *was* like. Then. I'm different now. I want different things. That's why I hired a private investigator to find your new address. That's why I dressed myself all up and drove a good two hours away from the nearest Nordstrom's in melt-your-makeup heat to find you."

"Two hours from Nordstrom's? You must be suffering horrible withdrawal," he quipped.

She thrust her fists onto her hips.

"I distinctly remember you regarding the grand opening of Nordstrom's as something akin to the Super Bowl, mister. We went together. You spent five thousand dollars on a suit in the first half hour alone." Her tone was even, but sharp. "Don't you dare condescend to me, Adam Brody."

Adam clenched his lips together. Her claim did indeed match what his sister had told him about the past few years of his life, as well as the facts he had solid proof of—like a whole closetful of designer men's wear languishing in the cabin's guest bedroom.

He raised his hands in surrender.

"I'm sorry."

Sydney sighed, then turned on a smile that just about outshone the sun.

"You're forgiven." She snaked her arms around his neck and pressed close, ignoring the sawdust and sweat clinging to his bare chest. Her breasts taunted him with soft pertness. Her scent enticed him. Her mouth, which she licked to an even glossier shine than her lipstick, begged for a kiss.

And who was he to make her beg?

He curled his hand around the small of her back and lifted her, pressing her lips to his. Immediately, her mouth opened, her hands reached up to grip the sides of his cheeks, her leg twisted around his thigh to bring the center of her sex in direct contact with his. Adam jolted with explosive need, dropping his other hand to her buttocks, crushing her closer until his body throbbed and his chest heaved. Wild sexual instincts overrode every ounce of sense he had. If not for Sydney pulling back, he might have stripped her naked right there.

"Whoa, sweetheart." She made short work of straightening her hair and clothes, tugging her tank top down so that her erect nipples drew his eye. "I remember we used to love the thrill of getting it on in the great outdoors, but don't you think we should find somewhere a little more private? I don't guess your sister would appreciate us screwing in her driveway."

Adam laughed. He'd never known a woman who spoke about sex so freely. Or at least if he did, he didn't remember her. Just like he didn't remember Sydney.

"We used to do it outside?"

Sydney rolled her eyes. "We were a hair away from being certified exhibitionists. Don't tell me you've already forgotten about our tryst on the roof of your building?"

"Unfortunately...yes."

"Excuse me?" She stepped back, clearly not believing him.

No time like the present to tell her the whole truth. "Much as I hate to tell you this...I don't remember us. In fact, I don't remember you at all."

3

"YOU'RE JOKING, RIGHT?"

Sydney searched Adam's face for any sign of facetiousness, but the sharp planes of his stubble-roughened cheekbones and the kiss-swollen curve of his mouth didn't show anything but dead seriousness. Even his irises, a unique light brown that reminded her of the fawn-beige paint on her father's first Rolls Royce, reflected nothing but honesty. They didn't twinkle with his notoriously wicked sense of humor. They didn't dart to the side when she persisted in staring.

"Tell me you're joking," she pleaded.

He glanced appreciatively down the length of her body. "I wish I was. You seem like someone who'd be hard to forget."

"Hard to forget? I'm impossible to forget!"

Sydney stepped back, teetering on her high heels, her toes straining against the razor-thin straps. Furious, she cursed and tore off the sandals. Her first instinct was to throw them long and hard across the lawn, but her second instinct—to throw them at his head—stopped her from throwing them at all. Ordinarily, she wasn't a violent woman. Instead of inflicting physical harm she decided to hold tight to the potential lethal weapons until she figured out how the hell Adam Brody, the man who'd almost made her break the dating mantra she'd lived by, could have forgotten their brief, but awesome affair.

"You're yanking my chain, aren't you?" She shook the shoes at him, hoping one more chance would convince him to change his story. How could he forget her? *Her?* "This is payback for my dumping your sorry ass."

Adam chuckled, and though the sound trickled through her like neat bourbon with a twist of lime, something sounded foreign to her. Un-Adam-like.

Her insides froze. She noticed a scar nestled in his thick eyebrows. She swallowed hard, her mind working furiously.

"What happened to you?"

"Accident, or so I'm told."

She dropped her sandals on the ground. Moisture deserted her mouth and she struggled to swallow, wishing she had that bourbon he'd reminded her of a second ago. With a tentative step, she closed the distance between them and brushed a lock of chestnut hair away from his forehead.

"Oh, God..."

"That's nothing."

He turned around and gave her a full, unhampered view of the still-red-and-puckered scar slashing down his back.

She gasped. "Does it hurt?"

"Sometimes. When it rains."

Tentatively, she reached out, but stopped with her fingers only centimeters away.

"You can touch it," he said. "It doesn't bother me."

Maybe not, but it sure as hell bothered her. Not because his once-perfect body had been marred by a deep, permanent mark, but because he'd been seriously hurt and she'd known absolutely nothing about it.

"When?" she asked.

"March twelfth, last year."

Sydney sucked in a breath. March twelfth? She'd left him on the twelfth, then jetted off to Scotland on the thirteenth. She remembered because it had taken quite a bit of coaxing from her publicist and agent to get her on a plane on such an unlucky day. Superstition hadn't been bred into Sydney, the daughter of pragmatic New England parents. But she'd somehow acquired the habit, most likely because she'd read mostly horror and paranormal fantasy books as a kid.

"That's the day I left. I mean, that night—I left you that night. It must have happened after…"

He turned, stretching his shoulders and neck. Then, tilting his head toward the side of the house, he directed her to the tire swing and a snatch of shade. He dug his hands into his pockets, but she didn't miss the way his arms tightened, as if he'd clenched his fists beyond her view.

"Renée thinks I went jogging, got hit from behind. I was wearing running clothes and shoes, though only one Nike Air was found at the scene." He got quiet, pointing Sydney toward the swing. Yes, her legs felt weak as they walked, but having never had something so basic as a tire to dangle from as a kid—her parents preferred a custom-built playset with Naugahyde fabric seats—she didn't feel compelled to indulge in that childhood pastime. Instead, she wrapped her hands around the chain and leaned for support.

"What time? I mean, I left pretty late."

Adam's eyes met hers and, for an instant, she recognized an expression of the man she used to know. His lids narrowed, slightly crinkling the taut skin at his temple. If she didn't know that men like him kept their brains well oiled, she imagined she could hear the gears working overtime.

"Sometime before midnight, because that's when the cops had a call about a body on the side of the road."

A body? Jogging? Sydney searched her memory, trying to pinpoint what time she'd left Adam's condominium, trying to figure out how the accident could have happened without her hearing about it, but she'd started shaking so hard, she could hardly breathe.

A body? Adam? God, he could have died. He could have been killed that night and buried and she never would have known. Something in her chest tore, and a hot wave of regret flooded her body. She glanced around, looking for a place to sit. The tire swing still looked gooey and black and forbidding, so she simply dropped down on the grass, knees first.

She'd barely settled onto her heels on the prickly lawn when Adam knelt beside her, wincing at the sudden downward movement.

"Are you okay?" he asked.

"Me?" She swallowed the lump of disbelief blocking her airway. He'd nearly died on the side of the road. That was why she couldn't find him when she'd returned from her trip. That was why he didn't remember her. "What happened to *you*?"

He looked down, causing a thick lock of hair to fall haphazardly over his eyes. He combed his fingers through the chestnut strands and Sydney's heart pounded faster. Such a simple, sexy act. Such a simple, sexy man. And he'd almost died.

"Not sure. The police report and doctors concurred that I was hit from behind. I didn't wake up from the coma for over a month, and when I did, I'd lost all memory of that night, as well as everything for about five years before."

She forced a grin, managing to quirk only half her mouth. "So I shouldn't take it personally that you don't know who I am."

He reached up and touched her cheek. The gesture might have cracked Sydney's heart another inch wider, but she realized he was only swiping away a bug.

"It took a few days before I even remembered Renée."

"But you remember her now," Sydney asked hopefully.

He shrugged again. "She's my sister. She's been around longer than five years."

Or six months.

"She's really protective of you," Sydney said, not wanting to dwell on the fact that despite his injury, it still hurt that he didn't remember her.

"She's the only person who thought I'd survive."

"I would have thought so! I would have...if I'd known."

Adam's mouth curved into a frown. "Why didn't you know? Why didn't Renée know about you? What were these *rules* you talked about?"

Sydney smirked. She supposed she should feel embarrassed or remorseful at this point—and she did. But not about the rules they'd—rather, she'd—laid out at the start of their affair. Her dictates had kept things neat, clean and had allowed her the illusion of organization in her dating chaos. The only thing that truly cued her normally inactive mechanism for regret was that her rules had kept her from finding out about Adam's accident. She'd created the rules to protect her heart from the distraction and inherent selflessness of love. She hadn't meant them to cut her off from providing help or solace to a friend.

"We had an agreement to keep things between us. *Only* between us," she answered.

"Why? Are you married?"

Sydney snorted.

His gaze widened. "Was I married?"

She rolled her eyes and smiled, amazed at his ability to kid about something so damned serious. While Sydney embraced a wide-open attitude toward casual sex, she drew the line at boinking another woman's husband. Best he knew that right up front. "The Adam Brody I knew was one-hundred-percent bachelor."

He shook his head. "Renée checked with my friends, all my employees in my office. No one mentioned you. Not even a hint that I had a lover."

Sydney stood up and swiped dry blades of brown grass off her knees. "When we agreed to keep things private, we did. It wasn't so hard since we lived in the same condo complex."

"You didn't see my sister sell the place? Move my stuff?"

"I left the next morning for Scotland and New England. I was gone two months. When I got back, your condo had been sold, your business was gone...oh, God, your business! That's why we'd gotten together that night! To celebrate some big deal. Jeez, what happened to the blueprints? The building?"

She watched his Adam's apple bob. At first, his lips tightened, then relaxed into a devil-may-care smile that didn't reach his eyes. Sydney tamped down a curse, her mind flying back to the night she'd left him—the night he couldn't remember. He'd been nearly giddy. Psyched. Like the quarterback of a football team who'd just thrown the winning pass and was simply waiting for his receiver to snatch the pigskin out of the air. No blockers. An open end zone. If Adam had been the dancing type, they might have waltzed all over his condominium to the sweet music of success.

Instead, they'd made love on the living-room carpet.

Hot moisture prickled between her legs as the memory rushed back. The minute the door had closed behind the courier who'd picked up the plans that would make Adam a multimillionaire, he'd ripped off her clothes and licked her skin from top to bottom. She'd laughed and screamed in shocked delight, allowing him his fun and her the pleasure, giving him complete control over the sex that night—never guessing their tryst would be the last.

He'd kissed every inch of her body, not slowly and teasingly like he normally did, but with hot, desperate need. The memory of his mouth on her made her nipples pucker, her skin flush. Her thighs clenched, recalling the way he'd thrust inside her and made her come.

"Maybe we should go inside," Adam suggested, snapping Sydney's eyes to his. "You suddenly look like you could use some of Renée's lemonade."

Sydney glanced down, wondering exactly how she looked. Thirsty? Horny? Hot? Maybe a finely mixed combination of all three. "Will she spike it with vodka?"

"If you ask nicely."

Most likely she'd spike the drink with Drano. But Sydney decided to keep her mouth shut and take whatever his sister offered. She had so much to process. And she couldn't think clearly while her libido overrode her brain.

With an almost inaudible grunt, Adam stood, helping Sydney with a hand on her elbow. She followed quietly, her shoes still dangling from her fingers, her mind swimming with questions and recriminations and sexual memories she hadn't realized she missed until she'd confronted the man who'd created them. He'd been unconscious for a month? Why did she feel she should have been there beside him, holding his hand? Whispering words of encouragement instead of traipsing all over the highlands with the private tour guide she'd seduced on her last night on the moors?

Why was a damned good question. Sex buddies didn't do the bedside thing. Sex buddies sent flowers, maybe a naughty card. And she and Adam had only been sex buddies—adult lovers with no other commitment to each beyond sexual exploration and pleasure. Yeah, he'd suggested they take their relationship to a deeper level, but she'd bolted, so certain that allowing herself to lose her heart would somehow destroy the life she'd worked so hard to build.

Then she'd finally realized, with the recent nudge from Cassie, that her life, ideal in some ways, sorely lacked in others. She'd initiated her search for Adam to try this relationship again. To give a good thing a real chance. Now she was a stranger to him. In fact, when she really thought about it, she'd been little more than a stranger for the six months they'd been lovers. And she only had herself to blame.

"Careful of that bottom step," Adam warned. "I need to refinish the wood."

Mindlessly, Sydney avoided the step he indicated, then promptly yelped as a sliver protruding from the next step slid into the ball of her foot. "Ow! Ow!"

"Aw, hell." Adam scooped her into his arms before she could protest and kicked on the screen door with his boot. "Renée, open up!"

His sister came running, her face a pale mask. "What? Adam, put her down! You shouldn't be carrying anyone so heavy!"

Amid the pain, Sydney grimaced at the insinuation. "I'm not exactly Shamu the whale, sister."

"Adam shouldn't be lifting anything heavier than live bait," Renée chastised, then turned her glare on Sydney. "You don't look like bait."

"Should have seen me when I was sixteen," Sydney shot back, trying to rationalize that though the pain throbbing in her foot made it feel as though she had a two-by-four shoved in the tender arch of her foot, it was likely only a good-size sliver. Besides, there was no way Adam could carry both her, slim though she was, and a plank of wood.

"Back off, Renée. Stop being a bitch. Sydney is hurt. Go get the tweezers and the first-aid kit."

He deposited Sydney on a comfortable—although worn—striped couch and knelt down beside her to take a better look at her injury.

Sydney swallowed a scream when Adam brushed his finger over the protruding splinter, sending a renewed wave of pain up her leg. She wasn't good with pain. She was a certifiable wimp, with a pathetically low threshold for discomfort.

Sydney protested when Adam brushed his fingernail over the splinter again. "Ow! Ow! Ow! Stop doing that! It hurts!"

"I'll bet it does. But I know pain. I think you'll survive once I take the splinter out and get some ointment on. Think you can suck it up long enough for that?"

Sydney couldn't contain a wisecrack, despite the ache in her foot. "If you remembered me, you wouldn't ask," she teased.

He met her stare, breaking into one of his heart-stopping smiles when she winked. Yes, she wanted him to catch the double entendre she'd made with the word "suck." Too bad Renée returned before he could respond.

"Here." Renée handed her brother the tweezers, then popped open the first-aid kit and slid it onto the couch beside Sydney. She remained quiet, but Sydney sensed a slump in her shoulders, as if Adam's chastisement had hit home.

"Can I get you a lemonade?" Renée asked, her tone surprisingly close to sincere.

Sydney smiled. Apparently, she wasn't the only woman in the room who had some sucking up to do. "That would be awesome, thanks."

Renée nodded and hurried out of the room.

"Was that a truce?" Sydney asked as Adam twisted her foot gently to the side so he could see what he was doing.

"Seems like. Renée doesn't like being called a bitch, particularly when she's acting like one."

"Bitch isn't always a put-down, you know. There's a whole movement that considers the word an acronym for Babe In Total Control of Herself."

Adam grinned as he tried to wrangle the tiny silver tweezers with his big male fingers. This was why men didn't pluck their eyebrows.

"I don't suppose you've been elected the spokes-model for that movement, have you?" Adam asked, his tone wry.

Sydney's spine straightened at the surge in her blood pressure. "Are you calling me a bitch?"

"See—no one likes it."

Just at that moment, he tugged the splinter free, giving Sydney two justifiable reasons to yelp.

He held up the tweezers, still holding tight to a half-inch sliver of wood. "Yeowch. I really need to refinish all those steps."

Sydney winced. The two-by-four had been removed, but her foot still stung like hell. She reached over and grabbed the ointment out of the first-aid kit.

"Here, let me."

Sydney considered protesting, then realized his hands felt good. Had Adam ever given her a foot massage? She couldn't remember, so she figured he must not have. There was nothing more noteworthy in a man's pampering repertoire than the ability to give a good foot massage.

He cleaned the wound with a cotton ball doused with hydrogen peroxide, then dried her skin with a square of clean gauze. His movements were gentle, but sure. His hands strong and hot. His fingers nimble. Long. As his touch trickled over her increasingly sensitive skin, she found herself staring in fascination at his clipped nails, bruised knuckles and sunbaked skin.

Images of him sliding his hands up her bare thighs flashed in her mind. He no longer had the smooth hands of an artist, with only small calluses from pencils and pens. His hands were stronger now, rougher. And so much more interesting.

"You seem to remember your first aid," she said, wondering if she should break the current of intimacy crackling between them. Or was the electricity all in her mind? All in her memory? All in her irrepressible libido?

Adam dabbed antibiotic ointment and then covered the wound with an adhesive bandage. He rubbed the ends in place, then continued to caress her with hard, intense strokes that lulled her muscles to instant relaxation.

She moaned.

"You have great feet."

He continued to soothe the balls of her foot with circular motions that destroyed her ability to sit up

straight. She sank back into the couch cushions and allowed his touch to ignite and kindle all the sexual
wants she'd planned to have sated today, before she
found out he didn't remember her. Before she discovered that he'd nearly died.

"You have great hands," she murmured.

"How great?"

She forced her eyes open enough to see the irreverent, wicked gleam in those almond eyes of his—the
same gleam she'd seen a hundred times before. Like
the night they'd made love on the terrace of her condo
while a party went on in the courtyard below. Or the
time he slipped a toe beneath her dress in a booth at a
restaurant, and, finding her pantyless, had brought her
to climax just as the waiter delivered another round of
drinks. They'd been risk-taking lovers, hedonistic and
selfish and adventurous.

Was any of that irreverence left?

He moved one hand to her arch, the other her ankle.
He smoothed and rubbed until hot shards of fire sizzled upward, making the center seam of her jeans too
tight against throbbing, intimate flesh.

"How great are my hands, Sydney?"

His calluses bit at her soft, pedicured flesh and she
snagged her bottom lip with her teeth to staunch her
moan. Even when he smoothed his fingers over her
calves, encased in jeans, she experienced a potent reaction to his intense massage.

"Your hands are awesome. Still too low, in my opin-
ion, but awesome."

He shifted, kneeling flush against the couch so he
could knead her thighs. He wedged his hips between

her knees, bringing her eye-level with a bare chest still glistening from the heat. She took a deep breath and lost herself in the spicy male musk sizzling off his skin.

"How's this?"

Sydney watched his gaze drop, watched the fascination intensify in his eyes, watched his mouth set in total concentration as he massaged her legs, his thumbs dipping lower and lower as his fingers worked their way higher and higher along her thighs—closer and closer to home. Every ounce of his attention was focused on his task, lulling her to complete relaxation.

He had one thing on his mind. And if that one thing was what Sydney suspected, she and Adam were about to have a very interesting afternoon.

4

A CUPBOARD SLAMMED in the kitchen, striking Adam with instant awareness of where he was—and of what he'd been about to do. He yanked his hands from Sydney's legs and rocked back on his heels, his body thrumming, every inch of his muscle and flesh intrigued and aroused.

"You don't have to stop," she told him, her voice throaty, deep. When her lashes fluttered open, only a thin, green circle remained around pupils black with need.

"My sister's in the other room."

"Then let's go somewhere private."

She didn't show a single sign of embarrassment that he'd almost committed a full sensual assault on her with his sister only a few steps away. Sydney's expression reflected only desire—the hot, unadulterated need to feel his hands on her body, no matter who might walk in on them.

"I don't know you," Adam said, certain the fact didn't bother him in the least, but he wasn't brain-damaged enough to think it might not make a difference to her. No matter how much of a bad girl she pretended to be—or truly was—he intended to play on the up-and-up.

She leaned forward, grabbed his hands and pressed

them to her rib cage. Her breathing wasn't quite as steady as she let on, and the moisture seeping through her paper-thin blouse testified to a heat more intense than the ninety-degree temperatures outside. She was burning up from the inside out, and she wanted him to know.

"You do know me, Adam. Better than any man ever has. You just don't remember right now."

A tinge of desperation clung to her tone, slapping Adam with a heavy hand of reality. He could only give her part of what she wanted—the part that had to do with his hands on her flesh. Yeah, he could give her sexual pleasure. He could give her a damned good time. But she'd already admitted that she'd come looking for him because she wanted what they'd once almost had—a real relationship. And that was outside his power.

Once his recovery had allowed him to live a semi-normal life, Adam had made some decisions. So long as he couldn't offer a woman a decent life with financial security and emotional depth, he'd sworn off dating altogether. The loneliness hadn't been easy, but he'd accepted the emptiness just as he'd accepted the excruciating pain of rehab. Until he found a new focus for his life, until he had a future beyond relying on his sister's business to give his life foundation, he couldn't commit to anyone. Not for a long-term relationship. Not when he had no way to predict where such an entanglement might lead.

"I won't ever remember, Sydney."

"You don't know for certain."

He winced, jabbed by the timbre of hope clinging to

her voice. He'd once held tight to the same kind of wishful thinking, but he'd been a pragmatist before the accident and struggling through recovery had made him one again. He wouldn't get his memory back. He'd never be able to draw again. And he'd never remember the intimate details of whatever explosive passion he'd shared with this intriguing woman, whom he wanted to kiss right here, right now, with every fiber of his soul.

"Yeah, I do know for certain." He pushed away and stood, marking a distance between them with the sharp sound of his work boots on the planked wood floor. "Why do you think I'm now making my way by pounding nails into precut wood instead of designing buildings and raking in the dough?"

She leaned forward, elbows on knees, thighs spread just enough to make his groin tug in response. "Because you look incredibly hot in jeans and a work-belt?"

"I'm serious, Sydney."

"I am, too, Adam, and that scares the crap out of me. I'm never serious. Serious is for people like my parents or my painfully responsible friends."

She stood and limped back into his personal space looking as cool as a white water lily floating on a rain-swelled pond. "But I'm serious about you and I'm not about to let your memory loss get in the way of what I want."

"Which is?"

She arched an eyebrow. "You, baby. Just you."

"I'm not the man you knew."

She licked her lips. "I don't know about that. Neither do you."

"I do know I can't make you any promises, Sydney. You remember what we once had. I don't. And the last thing I want to do is hurt you...or anyone."

Her lashes fluttered as she allowed her gaze to devour him. "I can take care of myself. And maybe a hot dose of me will jog that memory of yours. Worth a shot, don't you agree?"

Adam placed his hands on his hips to keep from pulling her into his arms and mussing her white blouse with the dirt and sawdust still clinging to his chest. She wore no bra beneath her tank top and, from so close, he could see the dark circles of her areolae, centered with tight tips that poked the soft cotton. Her eyes reflected pure want—with no fear, no expectations beyond the physical, though he guessed she harbored hopes he'd probably, inadvertently, dash. Still, how could any red-blooded American male say no to an offer like hers?

Renée strode back into the room with two tall glasses of lemonade, trying to look as if she hadn't heard any of their conversation. She stopped short, and he wondered if maybe she hadn't eavesdropped. His sister might be notorious for opening her mouth just long enough to either insert her foot or insult someone, but she'd focused on Adam and his recovery long enough to know the minute his emotions changed—mainly because he tried really hard and generally managed to maintain a steady calm of relaxed indifference. An impossibility with Sydney around.

"How's your foot?" she asked Sydney.

Renée handed Adam a glass, eyeing him with about a dozen unspoken questions—questions that probably had nothing to do with the state of Sydney's instep.

"Stings, but nothing I can't handle," Sydney answered, her tone friendly. She hopped back to the couch and accepted her glass with a smile. "I should know better than to walk around without shoes. If my mother were here, she'd be giving me that 'I told you so' look I so adore."

"Mothers love to be right about everything," Renée replied.

"Mothers?" he asked, stabbing Renée with a playful, accusatory stare. Sisters weren't so shabby at handing out bossy remarks, either.

"Where do you think I learned?"

Luckily, Adam did remember his mother. Sylvia Brody had been an enthusiastic mom, the kind who loved unconditionally and baked cookies and supported their father's authority. Luckily, Frank Brody had been a fair and even-tempered man who preferred his wife be the keeper of all strong opinions. Adam's move back to the family home after the accident, surrounding himself with loving memories, had been a positive experience.

The only downside was that because his parents had died only three years ago, he sometimes didn't remember that they were gone. He half-expected his parents to walk through the front door at any time. On the other hand, he held tight to primarily good memories. Which he needed. He'd had enough deep, dark times. More than enough. More than his share, at least in the past twelve months.

He needed a diversion. Preferably a sexy one like Sydney Colburn.

Renée scooted the rocking chair closer, the scraping sound snapping Adam into alert mode. "So, Sydney, tell me. *If* you and Adam were involved..."

Adam cleared his throat. "We were, Renée. I believe her."

Renée sat back, her feet planted firmly to keep the chair from moving in the casual, homey way it was intended. "Then why didn't she know about the accident?"

"That's complicated," Adam answered.

"No, it isn't," Sydney countered, then she stopped to think. He watched each detail add up into the complex story of their affair until she was nearly cross-eyed.

"Okay, I guess it is complicated," she conceded. "I'll summarize—we were involved, I left, now I'm back. End of story."

Adam coughed, trying to swallow a chuckle that bubbled up from some part of him that hadn't seen action in a heck of a long time. He considered himself a bottom-line guy. Apparently, Sydney Colburn had him beat by a country mile. "Not exactly the end of the story."

"End of that story, beginning of the new one," she said with a wink.

"It's not that simple," Adam countered.

"Why not?"

She had that look again. The same look of shock and disbelief in her sparkling emerald eyes that she'd worn when he'd confessed that he didn't remember her. He hadn't meant to make her look like that twice in one day. It wasn't a pretty sight. Actually, there wasn't much to Sydney Colburn that wasn't drop-dead gorgeous, but she had a sharpness to her eyes that would scare the living daylights out of any man with a brain enough to be afraid. Luckily for Adam, his brain was not only damaged, but the challenge of living with his sister had made him less likely to be intimidated by a strong woman.

"Adam needs to focus on his recovery," Renée said.

Sydney sat back so she had a clear view of him from head to toe. "He looks fine to me. Very fine."

She licked her lips again, then kicked up her appreciation by wiggling her eyebrows. Adam wasn't sure how much of her sexy reaction was for show, but he thought Renée was going to blow the vein in her temple.

"Adam doesn't need a woman like you in his life right now."

"A woman like me?" She drew her hand to her chest as if wounded. Man, if Sydney ever bottomed out in the romance market, she could take up acting. "That's a loaded statement. Care to elaborate?"

Adam jumped in. Man, these two women were going to drive him nuttier than a Snickers bar. "Renée, I can speak for myself."

"So speak," they said in unison, eyeballing each other with a showdown stare.

Adam stepped back, instinctively putting a safe distance between him and the two women. Despite their similarities—or perhaps because of them—they couldn't seem to get along for longer than ten seconds.

"I can't say I'm not interested in you, Sydney..." he began.

"Damn straight. You may have lost your memory, but I don't think you've lost your mind."

"No, apparently, my physical recovery has gone very well."

At the same time, he and Sydney glanced down at his crotch. Yep. He was good to go. Renée reacted by cursing the very foundation of their good Christian up-bringing.

"So what's the problem?"

Renée jumped in. "The problem—"

Adam interrupted his sister by shoving his empty glass into her hand. "I'd like a refill, Sis."

"What?"

"Now."

What a hell of day this was turning out to be, Adam mused. Renée snatched his glass, still half-full, and stomped into the kitchen. She banged cupboard doors and flung ice cubes into the glass so hard he was afraid she'd need the first-aid kit in a minute. But a man could only take so much catfighting before the appeal wore off, especially when the combatants were the sister he loved and a woman who fascinated him beyond reason.

"Renée's right, Sydney. I shouldn't get involved right now. It wouldn't be fair."

"Fair to whom? Me? I told you, I can take care of myself. I've been pulling off that trick for a long time."

"That may be, but you didn't come all the way out here to renew a no-strings-attached affair, did you?

You came here to try and start over, make what we once had mean something."

She opened her mouth to reply, then popped her lips closed just as quickly.

"Damn, I hate that," she finally muttered.

"What, when I'm right?"

"No, when I can't come up with a snappy comeback."

He laughed heartily, eliciting a reluctant grin from her. God, he could really start liking this woman. A lot. But getting involved right now wasn't the right thing to do. Not because he was fragile or still in need of physical recovery as his sister believed. But because he had nothing to give a woman like Sydney, at least nothing worth having for more than a few months' time.

Yeah, he had a job, but no career. He hadn't had time yet to figure out his direction, not when so many stumbling blocks remained in the tangled web of his past. Until Sydney had shown up today, he hadn't really allowed himself to think about finding out exactly what had happened on the night of his accident—he hadn't had a clue where to start. The police investigation had been one dead end after another. But Sydney had been in his condo with him shortly before he'd gone out running. Maybe she had seen someone, heard something. Maybe she possessed an insignificant detail that when added to the context of his accident and the vandalism at the office, might give him a place to start figuring out exactly what happened that night...and why.

After he'd come home from the hospital, he'd made the normal inquiries, using old contacts to see if his blueprints had shown up under another firm's design. So far, he'd received no feedback. But since he was no longer part of the industry, he couldn't be one-hundred-percent sure that the missing plans hadn't been stolen and sold elsewhere, perhaps in another country. With literally tens of thousands of architects and builders plying their trade all over the world, he'd had no logical place to start a real search—until, perhaps, now.

"Look, Sydney. I don't have the right, but could I ask you a few questions about what happened that night, before my accident?"

Sydney grabbed her shoes and buckled them around her slim, smooth ankles. "Sure, but I have a few questions for you, too."

"That's fair."

Renée must have finished pouring the lemonade by now, but she hadn't reappeared. He figured she was probably sulking and eavesdropping. Oh, well. If she heard anything she didn't like, too bad. He needed to do this. For his future.

"You start," he said, sitting beside her.

"Tell me about your recovery."

Adam grinned, realizing Sydney hadn't discounted his little sister's overzealous concern. When he'd told her about the accident outside, Sydney had been broadsided. That she cared about his health made him wonder just how shallow their affair actually had been.

"I had to learn to walk again, to do everything again, really. And I've had occupational therapy, so I can take care of myself. For the most part, I'm as physically recovered as I'm ever going be."

"What about your drawing?"

"Drawing?"

"Your architectural designs. You were going to be the next Frank Lloyd Wright."

Adam couldn't keep the disgusted sound out of his laugh. "That won't be happening."

"Why? You were an architect for longer than five years," she reasoned.

He nodded, his lips curled inward, his frustration severely tamped down in the deepest part of his gut. "My brain is different now. I remember the basics, the skills, but my visual perceptions are shot. I can't see things in the proper dimensions to draw anymore, not even with a computer."

Sydney forced a huge lump of pity down her throat. He'd loved his job with the same vigor that she loved hers. To lose her ability to write...the possibility stole her best words, leaving her with only, "Adam, I'm so sorry."

He waved a hand at her. "Hey, I'm alive. I have nothing to be sorry about."

Sydney admired his perspective, but she knew he had to mourn the loss anyway. Still, she wasn't qualified to be his therapist. Hell, she was hardly qualified to be his friend. They'd been lovers, end of story. And yet, she'd known about his obsession with his career. His single-minded ambition to become the next household name of building designers had been the quality that defined him.

Now who was he?

No wonder he was so reluctant to get involved with her again. His honorable side hadn't been damaged by the accident—which, unfortunately for him, made her want him all the more.

"What were you working on out there?" she asked, crooking her thumb toward the backyard.

"Renée designs custom playhouses for children. I build them."

Sydney smiled, amused to discover Adam now did something so whimsical, yet so sexy. I mean, what man caked in sawdust and sweat while wielding a hammer and nails for the sake of children didn't make a woman's pulse quicken? "Sounds like fun. I guess with you being independently wealthy now, you can do whatever the hell you please."

"Independently wealthy? Don't tell me your private investigator told you that, because if he did, you've wasted your money."

"'He' is a she, actually. And I'm not here for your money, I've plenty of my own, thanks. But, you know, she didn't find much financial information on you, except the sale of your business. You got way lower than I would have expected."

Adam stretched out his legs and shoved his hands into his pockets. "I took what I could get. I needed every red cent for my recovery."

He explained how his insurance hadn't covered some of the more experimental treatments that his sister insisted he have—treatments that helped him recover physically in record time. And now that he could no longer ply his trade as an architect, he assisted his sister with the business she had built from scratch—in the home their father had left them—with the carpentry skills he had taught them both.

Sydney listened, but couldn't understand. "But you'd just gotten that big multimillion-dollar contract!" she protested. "The one with the building that would revolutionize low-rise business structures. I mean, the timing couldn't have been better. Developers were clamoring for a way to avoid building more high-risk skyscrapers and then you finished your design. What happened?"

She watched him close his eyes and press his lips together in what could best be described as a reluctant wince, born out of pain not so much physical as emotional. "I'm not entirely sure. The plans to the building disappeared. All the backups were destroyed in what the police claim was a random act of vandalism."

"What do you mean, disappeared? All you had left to do was deliver the plans to the developer. You told me he'd set up an account with your money sitting ready for you."

"The plans were never sent."

"Of course they were! The courier came while I was at your place."

"What?"

Adam shot to his feet, but the floor beneath him rocked, as if a fault line had suddenly developed underneath the wet Florida soil. He knew the unlikeliness of that, so he forced himself back onto the couch. Shaking with a mind-numbing combination of confusion and shock, he grabbed her hands.

"What do you mean the courier came while you were at my place? The courier company said they received a cancellation call about ten minutes after my secretary placed the original order. They said they never sent anyone to pick up the plans. When Renée checked, the plans weren't in my apartment or in the office, which had been trashed, supposedly by vandals. The computer backups were destroyed. And the developer never received them."

Sydney sat back, and he could tell she was watching his face very carefully, as if she didn't know how he would react to whatever she was about to say.

Lucky for him, she seemed like a woman who didn't shy away from stress.

"The courier came, Adam."

"You're sure?"

"He came while I was at your apartment. I saw him take the plans. You wanted me to be there, so we could celebrate right after he left."

"Do you remember what he looked like? Do you remember his name?"

"I should," Sydney said, lifting his hands to her lips, placing a kiss on his knuckles, then winking with a sly grin. "I slept with the man only a few months before."

5

SHE DIDN'T SEEM the least bit embarrassed by her confession. In fact, she seemed downright amused. When she'd first pealed into his dirt driveway, cool behind the wheel of her Corvette, Adam had pegged her as a bad girl of the first order—or a clever wanna-be. Now he knew for sure.

Bad to the bone. Well, damn. Imagine the luck.

A bad girl might just be the type of woman he needed in his life right now. Someone open to possibilities. His existence had been damned serious lately. Cheating death. Losing the career he loved. A difficult physical recovery and lack of financial stability. But the restlessness Adam had fought since the moment he woke up in the hospital had grown to an unbearable state. Renée was the best little sister a brother could have, but she wasn't exactly schooled in the girls-just-want-to-have-fun department. His friends all had wives, children and responsibilities. Living in the boonies, he rarely saw his single city friends. Until now, he hadn't had the right motivation to venture out.

Sydney, on the other hand, didn't seem deterred in the least by the changes in his personality, which everyone he knew assured him were significant. She seemed less concerned with the fact that he'd lost his memory than with the insulting realization that he didn't remember *her*. Well, he was certainly open to the idea of getting to know her all over again, so long as she understood that he couldn't consider a serious relationship until he'd closed the chapter of his life regarding the accident and the missing plans. He couldn't redirect the path of his future when circumstances still trapped him in the past.

And as an added bonus, Sydney knew the identity of the courier who'd disappeared with his architectural masterpiece. The police, his colleagues, his sister— everyone he knew had encouraged him to stop torturing himself with the mystery of what happened the night he'd been hit by the car. Better to move on, they'd told him. Focus on his recovery. He'd done that, and yet he couldn't break from the prison of not knowing exactly what happened in the past. And subsequently, not knowing what he wanted to do with his life now.

At least, now he felt good. Damned good. And Sydney's hungry stare didn't hurt one bit.

"So you slept with the courier?"

"Well, not while I was sleeping with you. Right before. I was on this super-tight deadline and he came to get the manuscript just as I'd typed 'The End.'"

Her smile wasn't exactly wistful, but it was close.

"That book had a particularly lusty last chapter," she explained. "And, well, he was a hell of a good-looking man."

Adam's eyebrows popped up—of their own volition, since he hadn't wanted to give away his surprise.

"So he helped you work off a little sexual energy?"

"He wasn't bad. He wasn't you, of course, but he wasn't bad."

"That's good to hear."

"What, that he wasn't bad? I do try to be somewhat discriminating."

"I'm sure you do," he said, though he wasn't sure at all, "but I was referring to the fact that I was better."

"Oh, honey, I never thought I'd ever say this to a man and mean it, but you were the best."

"Are you trying to butter me up?"

"I'm telling the truth."

"What do you want from me, Sydney?" he asked, certain they needed to lay all the cards on the table right here, right now.

Sydney paused, grabbed one of the throw pillows Renée had lined up geometrically along the back of the couch and fluffed it to her liking.

"Well, you know, I have to reassess my answer. I came here for one very specific reason, but I wasn't acting on the full knowledge of what caused your disappearance."

"Damaged goods aren't so appealing, huh?" Adam wished he could have called back the sorry-sounding quip the minute it passed his lips, but when Sydney rolled her eyes, he was glad he'd been honest. Actually, he figured his habit of blurting out whatever was on his mind wasn't so much honesty as it was a drawback of hanging around Renée too much.

"Damaged? Please. Scars are sexy. I'll bet that nearly every hero I've written had a scar somewhere. I was referring to the nearly unbelievable fact that you don't remember me. That has thrown me for a complete loop."

Adam leaned forward, elbows on knees, aware that

Renée would give him another head injury if he put his dirty, sweaty back on her couch cushions.

"You sound like you're taking this personally. I don't remember any of the women I've dated in the past five years, unless I knew them before that."

Sydney fluffed her blouse, billowing air over her heated skin. Adam's gaze strayed to the curve of her breasts, the slim slope of her stomach, veiled by the filmy blouse so that he had to use his imagination to fill in the specifics. Even his brain damage didn't keep him from guessing the precise arc and weight of her breasts, the texture of her flesh, the precise placement of her navel. He glanced up to see if she knew he was ogling her, but either she was oblivious or simply didn't mind.

"Of course I'm taking this personally," she answered. "I've operated for years on the confident belief that I am completely unforgettable."

Adam chuckled. "Under normal circumstances, I'll bet you are. Unfortunately, nothing about me is normal."

Sydney leaned closer. The sheer blouse flared, allowing him a clear, unhampered view of her sweet-smelling skin.

"Normal is overrated."

Renée returned to the room, handed Adam his glass and then asked Sydney if she could refill hers.

"No, I'm fine, thanks."

Renée crossed her arms over her chest. "So, what did I miss?"

"You weren't listening on the other side of the doorway? I would have," Sydney admitted.

Renée coughed to cover a laugh, and Adam could swear he spied the telltale sign of respect in her eyes.

"I was in the bathroom."

Sydney's smile deepened. "Then you missed quite a bit. I would have held it. Seems I have something Adam needs, beyond the obvious."

Renée skewered Adam with a look that bordered on fear. "What is she talking about?"

"She knows the name of the courier."

"What courier?" Renée asked, frowning at Sydney's self-satisfied expression.

"The one who picked up the blueprints the night of my accident," Adam supplied, keeping his voice monotone, his tone even. Renée bristled whenever he wanted to discuss the possibilities of what had truly happened that night. The implications scared her. Once a happy-go-lucky, proud wearer of rose-colored glasses and a sunny outlook, his sister had become anxious, suspicious. The turning point had been their parents' deaths, but Adam had no doubt his accident hadn't helped.

Renée's once-innocent brown eyes rounded. "But the courier company said the pickup request had been canceled. They insisted no employee of their firm ever came to your condo or touched your blueprints."

"The courier company is full of shit," Sydney injected.

Adam nodded. That about summed it up.

"Do you remember what time he arrived?" Adam asked.

Sydney scrunched her mouth as she thought. "It *was* a year ago, and I did have other things on my mind besides what time the courier arrived. But it must have been before seven, because that's the last pickup time. We had dinner reservations at seven-thirty. We would have been on time."

"Would have?"

"We didn't quite make it." She wiggled her eyebrows.

Renée cleared her throat. "And you know for a fact that this guy worked for the courier company?"

"He wore the uniform, and I'm sure he'd worked for them previously." She turned toward Renée. "He did pickups from my condo all the time."

"Before that night, had he picked up recently at your place?" Adam asked.

Sydney bit her lip, reluctant to admit the truth. No, he hadn't. When she'd started seeing Adam on a regular basis, facing a former lover had seemed somehow...wrong. Instead of calling Kyle and explaining to him why she wasn't a sure thing anymore, she'd done drop-offs for her overnight documents, instead of requesting a personal pickup.

"I hadn't, if you'll pardon the expression, *used* him for a while, but I'd seen him around the complex. In his truck. I can't remember a specific date."

"Do you remember his name?" Renée asked eagerly, verifying for Sydney that she hadn't been listening while Sydney admitted she'd slept with the man.

"Kyle. He'd been with the courier for our area of town for over a year."

"Kyle what?"

She shrugged. "I don't know. We never exchanged last names."

Sydney considered that for a minute. Didn't quite seem equitable, did it? He'd known her last name. He'd had to, since her full name was on both the packages he delivered and the pickup orders. Once again, Sydney's rules of engagement hadn't worked out as effectively as she'd planned.

"Kyle is a good place to start," Renée said. "The courier company has to have records of their employees. We can find this Kyle and ask him what happened to the plans. Now we have a witness who saw him take the blueprints out of your condo. Adam, this could..."

Renée's voice died away midsentence. Sydney watched Adam's sister's enthusiasm wane as quickly as it had bubbled. Renée then slowly shook her head. Mirroring her concerned yet determined expression, Adam's face set grimly. The tension between the siblings simmered, thickened with each moment that passed.

"Maybe we shouldn't do this," Renée said finally.

Adam swore. "Why not? Don't think I can handle it, Renée?"

Renée flinched, and Sydney figured this was an argument they'd had before. "It's not that, Adam. The police advised us not to investigate on our own. I'll dig out that detective's card, give him a call. Maybe he can check into this Kyle person. Reopen the accident investigation. Maybe now, with real evidence—a witness— we can report a theft."

Adam shook his head as he turned away, his shoulders tight, his eyes slivers. "Whatever, Renée. I'm going to take a shower. Sydney, will you please wait?"

Sydney relaxed into the cushions of the couch and

took another long sip of lemonade. In the span of ten seconds, Adam's sister's reluctance had wound him tighter than the coil on a ballpoint. This was the Adam she remembered, even if he didn't. Driven, single-minded. Quiet in voicing what he wanted, but still planning on getting it without a doubt. Finding that aspect of his personality still intact spurred a thrill that shot to every pulse point in her body.

"I'm not going anywhere."

With drawn lips, he nodded and disappeared through a door she guessed led to his room. The minute the door clicked shut, she leveled her gaze at Renée.

"Okay, Sis. What's really going on here?"

Renée waved her hand, then collected Adam's glass. "It's none of your business."

"Says who? You?"

"You're real pushy, you know that? Less than an hour ago neither Adam nor I knew who you were, and now you think you're entitled to know our business?"

Sydney finished her drink and held the glass toward her hostess. "This has nothing to do with entitlement. I care about your brother. Took my losing him to figure that out, but I'm not so willing to walk away this time."

"The man you knew and the man you just met aren't the same person, Sydney. Not even close."

"He looks the same to me," Sydney said, hoping his sister didn't believe she'd have some hang-up about the man's scars. Sydney didn't mind so much if people pegged her as shallow; she'd be the first to admit she often operated with her own self-interest in mind. But, this time, something deeper was at play. Something she didn't quite know how to handle. But she'd driven all this way and dolled herself up—she wasn't backing down now. Particularly since this new Adam fascinated her just as much as the old one had. And she knew that, in his heart, he was exactly the same man she should have fallen in love with when he'd first given her the opportunity.

Now she would make her own second chance, even if she had to slap his sister out of her way to do it. But she'd try to reason with her first. She didn't need to make an enemy out of someone Adam cared about and who obviously cared about him. They might not ever be friends, but they could at least try to reach an understanding.

"I'm not talking about his looks," Renée answered.

"He told me about his visual dimension problems. I know he can't do architectural design anymore. I'm a wealthy woman, Renée. I don't want or need his income."

Renée slid onto the cushions beside her, her expression earnest, her fingers shaking so that she had to put the glasses down on the floor and wrap her hands into a ball. "It's not that, either. Sydney, Adam nearly died. The police ruled the accident a hit-and-run, but—"

"Hey," Sydney said, taking a chance and covering Renée's hands with hers. "I understand you're afraid to lose him. I totally admire your protectiveness. But Adam's a man, Renée. He needs to feel like one."

Renée dropped her chin to her chest and nodded softly, but after a few seconds tugged her hands free.

"Is that why you're here? You want to make him feel

like a man?" Venom dripped off Renée's words and Sydney's blood simmered.

She licked her lips and forced a grin. "If ever there was a job I was qualified for, that's the one."

Renée retrieved the glasses and shot to her feet, stalking across the room with an echo of anger in every step.

She swung to face Sydney just as she reached the doorway, which was adorned with a plaque that read, There's No Place Like Home. "Fine. I can't fight chemistry. Maybe screwing you will take Adam's mind off all that's happened to him. Go ahead and make him feel like a man. But if you hurt him—"

She didn't finish her threat, didn't need to. Either the claim would end up sounding empty or, at the very least, ridiculous. Sydney had no intention of hurting Adam. Not accidentally and not on purpose. She wanted him back. Even if she had to deal with his pushy sister on a frickin' daily basis.

Sydney didn't know if she was capable of loving a man—she'd never allowed herself to get close enough for fear of finding out. Until Adam. He'd been the only man in the long list of her lovers ever to challenge her status quo. She'd let him go once, but she wasn't about to make the same mistake twice. Not if she had half a chance of rekindling some of that lost magic.

So while she waited for Adam to shower, she devised a plan. She had something he needed—information. Not just a name, either—she knew what Kyle looked like. She doubted the courier company would be much help. With the litigious society they lived in, they weren't going to cough up one ounce of information without a warrant from the police or an order from the court. She'd read enough of her friend Devon's mystery novels to know that red tape in the police department and the court system could stretch for miles. But if you had the right friends, you could bypass some of the delay. Friends like Jillian Hennessy, her private investigator.

Sydney accepted Renée's wisdom of allowing law enforcement to follow up, but she also had plotted enough books with Devon to understand how the cops worked. This was an old crime. No hard evidence tied the theft of the plans—by the courier or anyone else— to Adam's hit-and-run. And robberies were often the lowest priority for overworked police departments. Before Sydney came along, Adam couldn't even prove to the police that someone *had* picked up the plans from his apartment. The cops might at least have jumped harder on the hit-and-run investigation had they at least known about Kyle.

She would encourage Adam to alert the cops when the time was right. For now, she suspected he needed to be a stronger part of the investigative process than just a victim calling in for occasional updates. She'd seen a glimmer in his eye—a hunger to take control, possibly for the first time in a long while. The man Adam had been before his memory loss would never have waited around to let someone else handle his problems. Adam Brody made things happen. He'd made his own success as an architect. Hell, he'd made Sydney rethink her entire philosophy of life.

Despite what she'd said to his sister, Adam didn't need Sydney to make him feel like a man—his strength ran too deep for even a life-threatening accident and memory loss to keep him down for long.

Yet if he needed reminding of his inherent male instincts, she could accommodate him—with pleasure.

6

ADAM STEPPED OUT ON THE FRONT porch just as Sydney slammed the trunk of her 'Vette. A slight limp told him her foot still smarted, but she'd put her heels back on, slung her little leather backpack purse over her shoulder and was now marching toward him like a woman on a mission. How any man could resist this woman, he didn't know. Not that she seemed to want men to resist her in any way, shape or form. He wondered how much of her casual attitude toward sex was real, and how much was meant to put the men in her world on edge.

He swallowed a grin, figuring that if he played his cards right, he would soon find out.

"You look...refreshed," she said.

He nodded. "You heading out?"

Sydney glanced over her shoulder at the car. "After I freshen up a bit myself." She climbed the porch steps with a saucy swing to her hips, her gaze sneaking toward his, to see if he was watching.

He made no secret that he'd watched every inch of her body. She made no secret that she liked when he watched.

"Do you feel—" she glanced brazenly at his groin "—up to coming with me?"

"You're a piece of work, Sydney Colburn."

She crossed her arms over her chest. "That's not an answer."

He chuckled and slung his hands into the pockets of his jeans. "An offer like yours doesn't require an answer. Where's my sister?"

Sydney shrugged. "No clue. But she did, sort of, give us a blessing to take off for a while. Said something about you needing a break."

Adam surrendered to the irrepressible instinct to touch Sydney's cheek, flushed from the sticky heat of the day. Actually, his instinct encouraged him to touch her in places much more intimate, but he figured they'd get there soon enough.

"I don't need her blessing."

Sydney laughed. "Yes, you do. You love your sister, and she loves you. She's just looking out for your best interests, that's all."

"My, you're magnanimous."

"Ha! Now there's something I've never been accused of before. I'll be right back."

She walked into the cabin as if she owned the place and Adam shut his eyes to enjoy the surge of electricity that shimmered through his body. What had started out as an ordinary, run-of-the-mill day pounding nails in the hot summer sun was turning into a very interesting opportunity.

When he'd first woken up in the hospital without his memory, what he'd done and who he'd known during those missing five years had been the least of his concerns. The ability to walk without help and breathe without a respirator had taken first priority. Once he'd mastered those skills again, he'd convinced Renée to fill in as many of the blanks as she could. Between her, his secretary and his friends, he'd learned that in the past five years, he'd become a career-driven maniac, focused to the point of obsession over a project that would revolutionize how companies utilized real estate for business properties.

Every other architect he'd ever known had wanted to create the next great skyscraper. Not Adam. He'd wanted to reinvent the low-rise, push design beyond bland business centers and, he shuddered, generic strip malls. It would be an Adam Brody masterpiece—architecturally innovative and fresh.

And then, over a year and a half ago, he'd finished the drawings and the 3-D, computer-generated models. He'd contacted the client who'd set up an account with a huge deposit, just waiting for him to deliver the plans. More money would follow when he supervised the construction. The design would not only ensure his fame among his peers and create a new, safer office environment, he'd be a wealthy man.

According to his secretary, Meg, he'd sent his staff home early after she'd called in the courier pickup request and, at his instruction, directed the company to fetch the plans from his condominium rather than the office. No one had known why he'd strayed from his normal procedure, but in light of the enormity of finishing the design, no one had questioned him. Now he knew why he'd wanted to go home. Or, at least, he could guess. He'd wanted to share his triumph with Sydney, his secret lover.

Until today, no one could tell Adam what happened between the time he had left the office at four o'clock and the accident around midnight. After receiving a phone call from Renée the next morning, his secretary had diverted to the hospital instead of going straight to work. At midday, she'd gone to the office to discover the place ransacked, their computer files corrupted, the 3-D models destroyed. The copies that she'd made of the blueprints and had locked in the safe had been missing, found days later nearly unrecognizable under layers of bleach. Renée, as Adam's next-of-kin, had ordered the woman to salvage what she could, file the insurance claims and police reports and close down.

But before Meg had left, his ever-efficient assistant had called the developer to ensure that the plans had arrived. They hadn't. According to Renée, Meg had nearly had a breakdown when she'd come to the hospital to deliver the news of yet another setback. Distracted and more concerned with Adam's recovery, Renée reported the theft to the police, told Meg not to blame herself and left it at that.

His chance to revolutionize architecture had vanished in one painful split second. His chance to make a difference in a profession normally focused only on making money had been run over and dragged down a rough stretch of highway for a half mile—just like he had.

Until today he'd had no idea what had happened after he'd left his office. Until today he'd had no proof that the courier had, indeed, fetched the plans. The knowledge changed the entire dynamic of his complacency with his new life—making playhouses with his sister, living life one day at a time, forcing himself to remain content with what he had, rather than what he could have had or what he'd lost.

She probably hadn't intended to, but Sydney had changed the entire focus of his existence. Not only had she filled in a few of the blanks, she'd also lit a fire deep inside him that made his homey cabin and monastic existence anathema to his once-predatory nature.

Yet, while she hadn't inspired one single solid memory of who he used to be, she'd certainly stirred up erotic impressions and basic instincts he could no longer ignore.

Adam Brody was a man who took what he wanted.

And he wanted Sydney Colburn.

When she emerged from the house, her wavy shoulder-length red hair had been captured in a sassy ponytail, damp wisps of auburn curling around her face. She looked primped and powdered and ready to take on the world, though Adam suspected Sydney wouldn't be any less sure of herself even if she looked like she'd just emerged from thirty-nine days on *Survivor*. Of course, this was just a suspicion. Except for finding out more about his missing plans, he couldn't think of anything that intrigued him more than discovering every nuance of what made bad-girl Sydney Colburn tick.

"Ready to go?" she asked, walking toward her car.

"Where?" he asked, leaning on a porch support beam.

She glanced over her shoulder, her expression startled. "Does it matter?"

With his amnesia, surprises came on a daily basis. He frowned and remained on the porch, causing her to stalk over, grab his hand and yank him along behind her.

"Men!"

"What would you do without us?" he asked, heading toward the passenger door. He had to divert his grab for the handle to catch the keys she threw his way.

"Here's hoping I'll never have to find out," she replied.

"I can't drive, Sydney," he said simply, tossing the keys back.

She caught them with one snatch, then lobbed them to him again. "You got a license?" she asked.

In his wallet, which he'd tucked in his back pocket. He'd just gotten the medical okay to drive again, so, legally, he could get behind the wheel of a car.

Morally was a whole other matter.

Sure, he'd driven Renée's battered truck to the hardware store or up to the gas station, but the pickup was probably worth about a buck fifty at the junkyard. If he lost his concentration and wrapped it around a tree, there was no great loss. Sydney's mode of transportation was a Corvette. A sleek speed machine. The hottest star in a teenage boy's wet dream—besides a sexy, lusty babe riding shotgun.

If he drove, he'd have both the car and the babe to worry about. But his palms itched to grab the wheel, and he hadn't realized he'd licked his lips expectantly until Sydney laughed, opened the passenger door and pushed him to climb over to the driver's side.

"Welcome to the world of the living, Brody."

"Have I ever driven this car before?"

Sydney's grin was curved with mystery. "Get behind the wheel. Rev her up. See if the feel brings anything back."

SYDNEY WAS NOT A DOCTOR. Nor was she a psychiatrist. She'd dated an M.D. once, but, for the most part, gave shrinks a wide berth. For obvious reasons. Poking into her screwy psyche could cause permanent damage—to her *and* to the exploring psychiatrist. On the surface, she could be the poster child for the poor little rich girl stereotype—raised in a relatively cold, wealthy family, the recipient of a large trust fund, exposed to the mind-altering experiences of cotillions and coming-out parties at a painfully young age.

So Sydney had decided around age twenty-one to stop trying to live up to everyone else's expectations and do whatever the hell she pleased. She shunned the acting and took up the gauntlet of free living and embraced all she could be. She lived in the moment, used her talents to the best of her ability and saved the psychology for the creation of her fictional characters.

And who knew more about amnesia than a romance writer? A character with a lost memory had been one of the most popular romance gimmicks since the virgin bride and the avenging sheik. What hadn't been dissected in books had been exploited on the soaps, one of the few indulgences Sydney didn't readily admit to, except to Devon, who shared her passion for *General Hospital.* So even though she didn't have a medical degree, she knew a little more than most about the condition.

More than likely, Adam's memory loss was permanent. Miracle recoveries after serious head trauma, particularly when coma was involved, were mainly the stuff of fiction. But Sydney didn't much care if Adam remembered what she'd offered him for breakfast on his birthday a year and a half ago—strawberry crepes served on her bare belly—so much as she wanted him to remember *her*. Anything about her. Anything about them. Just one little thing would do.

She watched him glance her way once or twice during the trek over the interstate and not once did she see that spark of recognition she wanted. And it didn't take a shrink to figure out why she so desperately needed him to remember her.

If he didn't recall anything about her—about them— she had no foundation on which to build the deeper relationship she wanted with him. She'd have to start over, from scratch, make him like her all over again. When he'd invited her to stay the night a year ago, he'd challenged her to reexamine their affair in a way that made her suspect he'd already begun to fall in love with her. Now he had no memory of his feelings, setting her back to page one.

"How's it feel?" she shouted, the speed sheering the sleek car with wind.

"Handles like a dream," he shouted back.

"Yeah, a wet one."

Adam spared her a flash of surprise, but she suspected it wasn't because she'd said something crude, but because she'd probably said exactly what he'd been thinking. The evidence shone in his naughty smile.

"So remembering to drive is like riding a bike, huh?" she asked.

"Seems so."

Hopefully, driving a car wouldn't be the only physical talent he hadn't lost to the accident.

They drove in relative silence for about an hour, chatting about the weather, laughing about the wind, bitching about the traffic as they drew closer to Tampa. Sydney directed Adam to the south side of town, to a nondescript, blond-brick office building shrouded by hundred-year-old oak trees and prickly Sago palms. They parked in a shady spot near the door.

"What is this place?" Adam killed the engine and tossed Sydney the keys. "I thought you were taking me somewhere interesting."

Sydney slapped the keys into her purse and got out of the car. "Don't judge a building by its exterior. You'd never guess what depraved and fascinating practices occur inside."

She waggled her eyebrows. Adam's frown showed every ounce of his skepticism, though it was softened by a grin that indicated he hadn't lost his sense of humor and would play her game, at least for a little while.

She latched on to his arm as they followed the walkway to the front door, a single glass panel. In three-inch-high gold, cursive letters read, "The Hennessy Group."

Adam paused at the door. "Sydney, why do I have a sinking suspicion you're about to lead me into trouble?"

She masked her face in complete innocence. "Me? Trouble? If I didn't know you'd forgotten me, I'd be insulted."

"Yeah, right. What is the Hennessy Group?"

"You'll see, Adam, sweetie...you'll see."

TEN MINUTES AFTER LEAVING Jillian Hennessy's office, Adam decided that Sydney Colburn was a woman to watch, carefully, the way he watched gators who came up from the river to sunbathe near his work area. Like the fascinating reptiles, Sydney had scary friends. He'd followed her into the offices of the Hennessy Group expecting from the decor and the atmosphere that she'd taken him to visit her accountant.

Then, they'd gone beyond the tasteful but bland reception area, past the cluster of paneled, cozy conference rooms into a collection of offices he would best describe as an inner sanctum. Machines and gadgets whirled and buzzed. Walls flickered with television screens and flat LCD monitors. Smartly dressed people sat in front of top-of-the-line computers, their ears hooked into headsets, their fingers flying over keyboards. It looked like the Hollywood version of the CIA or the Justice League.

Then he'd met Jillian Hennessy, a partner in the Group. At the time, he couldn't believe his luck—two sexy redheads in one day. Jillian was married, though, or so said the small emerald and opal band on her finger and the nameplate on her desk that read, Jillian Hennessy Lawrence. When Sydney introduced Jillian as her favorite private investigator, Adam's fascination with Sydney ricocheted up a notch.

Without being asked, Sydney had decided to help him sort out the mystery of his accident. He figured there'd be a price to pay—but he couldn't imagine Sydney asking for anything he wasn't ready, willing and able to give.

She spared no details, filling Jillian in so the private investigator could use her expertise to help him. After Sydney told her about the courier and the missing blueprints, Adam gave her the name of his former assistant and the client who'd commissioned the plans. He'd told her about the accident and how now, with Sydney's information, he wasn't so sure the theft of the blueprints and his hit-and-run were as unrelated as the police insisted. He still had no real proof, but his instincts were impossible to ignore.

In little less than an hour, Jillian warned them to be careful and lie low, and then she sent them on their way, promising to have something for them by the next morning. In the meantime, they had the rest of the day with nothing important to do but get reacquainted with the town where he'd once lived—the setting of their torrid love affair.

This time, Sydney took the driver's seat in the 'Vette.

"How long has it been since you've been by the condo?" she asked after revving the engine and easing the car out of the lot.

At last, an easy question. One that didn't make his head pound or elevate his blood pressure because he couldn't remember the answer. "I haven't been back at all. After the vandalism at the office, Renée got spooked and had the condo cleaned out and sold in record time."

Sydney pressed a little too hard on the brake at the stop sign, jerking them to a stop. "Renée suspected foul play from the beginning? She didn't say anything about that. I thought she just didn't want you to leave with me."

Adam grinned. "I'll bet she didn't. She's never *said* she suspected a connection between the vandalism, my accident and the missing plans to me, either, but I know my sister. She reads a lot of suspense novels. She's one of those 'worst-case scenario' people."

"She seems older than you," Sydney commented.

He'd noticed it, as well. Though Renée was six years his junior, her overprotectiveness made her act and look much older. He had no one to blame but himself. He'd been the reason she'd become so tenacious about his health, so responsible for the weight of the world.

"She didn't always. My mother used to worry because Renée always seemed to have her head in the clouds."

Sydney swiveled in her seat, her expression both doubtful and curious. "What changed her?"

"My accident was probably the final nail in the coffin, but she was really devastated when our parents died. She was supposed to have gone with them, but changed her mind at the last minute. There was a fire in their hotel. The investigators initially ruled the blaze as electrical, but Renée never believed that. She pushed hard for more examination. Turned out a disgruntled employee set the fire."

"God, that sucks. I'm sorry. About your mother and father. Your sister, too. My parents drive me crazy, but at least they're here to enjoy my insanity."

Adam chuckled at her comment, but found her lack of previous knowledge about this crucial event in his past hard to understand. "I never told you my parents were dead?"

"You never told me you had a sister. We never shared those things."

"Part of our 'rules'?"

She didn't answer, but shoved the car into gear and took off as quickly as she could down streets paved with brick. He remembered the area, Hyde Park, because he'd worked at a firm here early in his career, just after his apprenticeship with Malcolm and Associates in Baltimore. Even with the missing chunk of years, Adam still had most of his past. Glimpses that, fortunately, didn't include the grief over his parents' tragic deaths in Las Vegas, during one of the only vacations from their simple rural life. But while he didn't remember the event, he lived the aftermath on a regular basis. No mystery surrounded why his sister had become a bulldog about his safety, particularly after his accident, which also had troubling circumstances.

"So Renée gave her blessing for us to take off together, huh?" he asked. "How did you manage that, anyway?"

Sydney slipped her car into fourth gear and merged onto the interstate traffic. "When I want something, I get it."

Birds of a feather. "And you want me?"

Her smile split her face in two. Her eyes sparkled with mischievousness, her mouth curved in expectation. "Can I assume the desire is mutual?"

"You're not exactly a tough sell, Sydney. You're sexy, smart, generous," he said that word last, not certain she'd take it as a compliment. She only raised her eyebrows. "What's not to want?"

"Tell me something I don't know, Adam. But I do want more from you than just sex."

From what Sydney had told him about herself and from what he'd observed in the past few hours, he couldn't imagine Sydney playing with a hidden agenda. He knew when she'd first shown up at the cabin, she had come looking for him to rekindle their affair on a more emotional level. She'd admitted his memory loss had changed her agenda since then, but she hadn't yet confessed what her new expectations entailed.

"More than just sex? Care to clue me in?" he asked, truly and utterly intrigued.

Her laugh latched on to the wind slicing through the speeding car. She didn't answer with words, but from the look in her eyes, Adam figured he was in serious trouble.

And, damn, trouble had never felt so good.

7

SYDNEY PULLED INTO the covered parking garage beneath her condominium and killed the engine, sitting for a moment before glancing over at Adam, who seemed totally unaware of the significance of their surroundings. He unfastened his seat belt, then stared at her, waiting. She peered through the windshield, then over the back seat. He did the same. She glanced over at the elevator, the balcony, the winding open-air staircase that led to a walkway between his old building and hers—officially, the place where they'd literally first bumped into each other.

Nothing.

"No bells ringing in that head of yours?" She didn't want to assume that his blank look meant what she expected.

He looked around again, leaning back so he could see past the elevator and the thick concrete supports.

"Are we somewhere important already?"

She rolled her eyes. "Duh."

"It's a parking garage."

Maybe to a guy who'd lost his memory of the past five years that's all it was. To her, it had been the first public place where they'd made love. The memory seemed so fresh to her, the daylight shining in from outside dimmed in her mind to the sultry hour past midnight, when they'd returned to the condo after a dinner on the beach. He'd been at the wheel of the 'Vette as they'd cruised over the bridge, trying to keep his eyes on the road while she'd unzipped his pants and stroked him until he was hard as a rock. At the first stoplight, he'd repaid her by slipping his hands beneath her dress and coaxing her to orgasm. Only the cop car idling beside them kept her from screaming out her pleasure and they'd almost gotten a ticket for staying too long in the intersection after the light had turned green.

After they'd arrived in the garage, they'd tried to make it back to either his condo or hers, but pure animal lust had won out. They'd done the deed right up against the concrete pillars. The experience had been forbidden, thrilling. Unforgettable.

And he didn't remember, darn him.

Sydney surrendered. "You're right. It's just a parking garage." And what they'd done there had just been sex. Maybe that was the problem. Maybe she needed to bring him back to a place where they'd shared something more significant. Trouble was, they'd done everything in their power never to share anything more significant than mind-shattering orgasms and a wicked good time.

Well, Sydney had her work cut out for her—first, trying to inspire him to remember, and second, creating new memories to replace the lost ones. Luckily, she looked forward to both tasks.

"I know the new owners of your place. Your sister must have sold the condo furnished because they hadn't changed much last time I stopped by. If you want to get in, look around, I can give them a call."

Adam nodded, but his expression was noncommittal. "Sounds like a good plan."

She unbuckled her seat belt. "Let's go up to my place, first. I'll call from there."

He helped her put the top up on the car, then followed her into the elevator. The condominium complex consisted of four buildings, each with two levels of private assigned parking below two levels of condos. Holding only four condos per floor, the buildings were arranged so they formed an intimate quad around a heavily landscaped courtyard complete with a pool, hot tub, wet bar and cabana. The condominiums looked as expensive and exclusive as they actually were. Sydney had been one of the original owners, and had made a large sum of money from buying several other units when she'd bought hers. With the condo's desirable reputation jacking up the price, she'd resold them for a tidy profit—enough to completely pay off her mortgage.

Her condo was actually two units, top and bottom floor, connected by the sexy spiral staircase her builder had insisted was frivolous at worst and retro at best. She remembered that Adam, upon his first visit to her place, had complimented her choice. She unlocked the door with her key, then punched in the security code, wondering what he'd say this time. He hung back a few steps and she watched him study every detail as they walked inside—as if the decor might be the ticket to jogging his memory.

She closed the door behind him. The dim sunlight,

slowly succumbing to sunset, pressed a lavender hue over her ivory leather couch and shimmery pearl walls. She flipped a light switch, igniting a series of lamps beneath her treasured eclectic collection of art. Two Tarkay original oils on canvas. A Chagall. Several assorted lithographs by currently unknown artists she had high hopes for. And, of course, her posters.

"You're a big Mae West fan," he said, slipping by the framed movie advertisement for *My Little Chickadee*.

"Every woman should be," she answered. "For that matter, so should every man."

"Not all men like bad girls."

She laughed. "Oh, yeah? Name one."

He chuckled and slung his hands into his pockets. In the shadowy light, she couldn't tell if he was just being casual and comfortable, or if he had something hard to hide.

"Then you think every woman should be a bad girl like you?"

Sydney crossed her arms loosely, trying to remain nonchalant as he strolled nearer the staircase, which was hard to see without many lights on. "I don't preach. I don't recommend my lifestyle to anyone, because, frankly, I don't give a damn how any other woman lives her life. But I enjoy myself. When I die, I'll have no regrets."

Adam nodded, making Sydney wonder what he was thinking. In the past, she wouldn't have wondered. She would have squelched her curiosity by reminding herself that if he didn't like the choices she'd made, he knew where the door was. But that was before. Before she'd realized that she'd missed out on a chance to create something meaningful with Adam. Before she'd learned how he could have died on that road outside the complex, the one she'd carefully maneuvered to avoid on the way home tonight, choosing an alternate route to the main entrance that bypassed the main thoroughfare.

Now she wanted him to remember her, not the hit-and-run.

How he judged her could make the difference between reconnecting with him on a deeper level or losing him forever. The truth rankled, but she shrugged it off. Sometimes, reality sucked.

"Does my life philosophy bother you?" she asked.

He thought for a minute, then countered, "Was I a judgmental ass before the accident?"

She laughed. Next to her, Adam had been the premiere purveyor of the live-and-let-live lifestyle. "Not in the least."

"Then why start now?"

"I'm just wondering if the only reason you're here is because I'm going to help you find your missing plans."

Adam crossed the room in quick, purposeful strides. Before she could register the depth of the expression on his face, he entwined her in his arms and swept down, locking his lips with hers. His arms cradled her with such power, she felt her entire body relax, trusting him to keep them both upright while she surrendered to the sheer pleasure of the kiss. Tongues dueled and tasted. Hands roamed. In an instant, the filmy blouse she'd worn over her sexy tank top floated to the floor. He'd unbuttoned the top of her jeans, skimming hot fingers just inside so that her tummy skittered with hot wanting. She explored just as desperately. So much to relearn. So much to lose. His arms were thick with muscle, his chest tight with need, his sex bulging against the seam of his jeans. When he pulled back and nibbled her neck, precisely on the spot just beneath her earlobe that always drove her insane, she let a flash of hope skitter across her mind.

"Okay, you're here for the sex, too," she said, unable to keep the quip inside.

"You did offer," he answered, his almond eyes teasing, his mouth working its way across her bare shoulder.

"Yes, I did. I most certainly did."

He ended his path of kisses with an erotic lick across her knuckles. "And I intend to take you up on that offer, and maybe sweeten the pot myself. But first, let's check out my old condo. When we make love, the only thing I want to be thinking about is you."

He released her, kissed her one last time on the temple, then strolled over to the large bay window overlooking the pool. Sydney took a few seconds to remind herself where she was and what she was supposed to be doing. Oh, yeah. The phone. Call the neighbors. Quick. And then, judging from Adam's confident, cocky tone, prepare for the seduction of a lifetime.

NOTHING. Adam walked out of the condominium disappointed, almost forgetting to turn around one last time and thank Sydney's neighbors for letting them inside. He shouldn't have gotten his hopes up. Shouldn't have allowed Sydney's enthusiasm to bubble over into his resigned heart. He wasn't going to remember the past five years. The best he could do was figure out who now had possession of his architectural plans and then work to restore the wealth that should have been his as a result of his hard work.

But he couldn't do that tonight, so he was going to concentrate on what he could accomplish—seducing Sydney Colburn.

More and more, the woman fascinated him. Her humor bordered on irreverent, her intelligence skated the line between brilliant and genius. She thought fast and lived faster. Add to that her incredible beauty and inherent sensuality and a man could do no better.

So why hadn't he captured the lady's heart before? Why had she walked away when he'd tried to take their relationship beyond the boundaries they'd set up? He wondered if that mystery haunted him more than the identity of the driver who'd crashed into him or the current location of his blueprints.

But tonight the only mystery he had a shot at solving dealt with Sydney. Before they stepped into the elevator to go back up to her condo, he grabbed her hand and tugged her close.

"Let's go somewhere," he suggested.

"Where?" she asked, her eyes flashing with interest.

"I don't know. Somewhere special. Somewhere you've never been with any other man but me."

"That's a tall order," she joked, but this time he felt relatively certain she was exaggerating.

"Indulge me."

She pulled her car keys out of her pocket, detached her condo keys, then tossed him the ring that would start the Corvette. "My pleasure, but I'll need to run upstairs first. Warm up the engine. I won't be two minutes."

She didn't lie. Though it had felt like an hour, Sydney flew upstairs and then back down in less than one hundred and twenty seconds. She had her purse in one hand and a small cooler in the other.

"Let's blow this joint," she instructed, green eyes flashing. She tore her hair out of the ponytail and as they raced out of the garage, the wind swept her curls into a flowing mass of sexiness.

She gave him directions, and in less than ten minutes, they'd apparently arrived. When they approached the back entrance to what appeared to be a country club, she leaned over and flipped off the headlights, then extracted a key card from her purse.

"I take it you're not a member," he asked, trying to concentrate on something besides the way she wiggled her backside as she climbed across his lap to reach for the automatic gate.

"Yeah, right. Do I look like a debutante?"

"I don't know any debutantes."

She slipped the card into the machine, and after a red light turned green, a buzz alerted him that the gate had slid open.

"Believe me, none of them look like me, talk like me or act like me. I used to date the head groundskeeper."

He hesitated before easing the Corvette through.

"Then you've been here with him?"

Sydney grinned. The fact that he'd exhibited even the least bit of jealousy seemed to please her, but he wished he could restate the question.

"Not the way I've been here with you."

He scowled, so after laughing and insisting he go through the gate before it slid closed, she explained further. "The head groundskeeper is a closet gay. But we work out together at the gym and when he needs a date, he calls me. In return, he gave me a copy of his key card and showed me this entrance."

"Why?"

"So I could seduce you outdoors."

"You needed a private country club for that?"

She settled back into her seat, her eyes and smile dancing with that blatant naughtiness she wore so well.

"Just wait. You'll see."

After spying her check her watch, Adam followed her directions down a thin path, past a small outbuilding and into a clump of trees. In the distance, a large colonial mansion at least three stories tall, lit by countless lights, loomed on a small, man-made hill. He saw no one milling about the expansive verandah or ornamental garden, but guessed the humid air kept the club members inside where the air-conditioning could protect their hundred-dollar hairdos and even pricier clothes.

Sleek greens and brushed sand traps dotted the pristine landscape. Palm trees lingered on the edges, mixed in with native pines and palmetto. Adam had never been an avid golfer, but he'd learned the game from his onetime mentor, Marcus Malcolm, so he could work the links for business. With a high handicap and little patience for the slow-moving sport, Adam finally convinced Marcus to leave the golf-related schmoozing to his son, Steven, the heir to the Malcolm design firm and a much better golfer. With or without his amnesia, Adam couldn't remember the last time he'd been on a green, and he was certain he'd never snuck onto a green late at night, except maybe once when he was a kid, filching lost balls to sell back to golfers for bubble gum money.

The minute Sydney pointed to where she wanted him to park, a forbidden thrill hit him full force. Sliding the car between two small hills, and with it camouflaged from behind by a clump of bushes, he knew no one could possibly see them.

They'd be in the dark, but out in the open.

Amazing.

When he pulled the emergency brake, she jumped out of the car. She'd already discarded her shoes and wore nothing but the midriff-baring tank top and her jeans, which were unfastened. Tiny brass buttons, now folded down just under her navel, caught a flash of moonlight and winked.

He didn't need any more invitation than that.

He chased her out onto the lawn, catching her as she spun, bringing her down to the ground with a soft thud, his arms cradling her fall. Laughter peeled against the quiet of the night—his deep, hers light. An invigorating rush coursed through him, compelling him to capture her mouth with his and kiss her long and hard.

Her scent, a romantic mixture that reminded him of sunrise—crisp and cool, softened by the colors of lavender and rose—blended with the fresh scent of the grass into an intoxicating combination. He inhaled as he nibbled her neck, fired by the sound of her laughter, invigorated by the way she moved her body so his sex pressed into the juncture between her thighs.

"God, I want you, Sydney," he admitted, not knowing when he'd wanted someone more than he did at this moment.

"Then take me, Adam. That's why we're here."

He kissed her thoroughly, his tongue and lips learning her mouth, his hands blazing a trail down her sides, across her back. She was bold and brazen, stopping only once to wiggle out of her white-washed jeans so that she wore only her tank top and purple T-back panties. The tiny straps crisscrossed her hips and thighs, fairly begging for removal with his teeth.

He moved forward, until a thought struck him. Had he done that to her before? Had he taken off her underwear that way, or had the scenario popped into his mind only because it was perfect for the moment?

He pulled back.

"What?" she asked.

"We've made love out here before, right?"

She scrambled onto her knees, her eyes filled with contained expectation. "Do you remember?"

"I'm not sure. I have a very strong image of me removing your panties with my teeth, but I don't know if it was a memory or an impulse."

She rolled her eyes, then playfully let herself fall to the side, her arms reaching out to him. "Well, damn, Adam, I can't remember all the little details! You're going to have to recall something a tad more significant."

He crawled over to her, like a jaguar on the prowl.

"Then I'm going to have to do something more significant."

"Go right ahead."

First, he was going to make his fantasy real. Memory or not, he wanted her panties off and he wanted to feel the scrap of fabric between his teeth before he tasted her. He couldn't help but growl just before he pressed his lips to her instep and then kissed a hot path up her calf, over her knees and across her thigh.

As he neared her panties, her scent intensified—muskier, hotter, wetter. He dipped his nose over the small triangle of material, filling his senses with her until his own jeans cramped around his groin and his shirt grew moist down his back. Reclined on the swell of a small hill, he glanced up to note the soft shadows of bliss playing over her face—eyes half-shut, mouth half-open, nostrils flared and breathing unsteady. She'd fanned her hair behind her, framing her glistening skin with strands of fire. She wore no bra beneath the T-shirt, so her nipples pebbled high and hard. His mouth watered to suckle them, and he would.

Very soon.

First, the panties. The moment he tugged at the scrap with his teeth, she lifted her hips, her knees bent. He dragged the silky material down, baring her sex to him like a present wrapped in satin. He unhooked the panties from her ankle, then tossed them aside, the first layer of clothing soon buried beneath his shirt, his jeans and his briefs. Then, he realized he didn't have a condom.

He swore. No getting around safe sex with their combined histories.

She leaned back on her elbows, her expression soft with wanting, but amused with that sassiness he'd forever associate with Sydney Colburn. "Check the glove compartment. I'm practically a Boy Scout, I'm so prepared."

"There's nothing boyish about you, lady," he rumbled, then jogged back to the car, hating to lose sight of her for even an instant. But after fumbling with the latch, he tore through the collection of audio tapes, car manuals and fast-food napkins until he found a plastic baggy filled with over a dozen foil packets.

Holding the baggy to the light from the dash, he couldn't make out which one he wanted. What the hell. For all he knew, they'd need them all. After a quick glance in her trunk netted him a blanket, he closed the car door and shot back to their private little hill.

But Sydney was gone.

8

SYDNEY SLIPPED AROUND the corner of the gardener's shed, turned the timing mechanism and then flipped the switch in the control box. She slipped back along the narrow path in time to see Adam emerge into the light, naked and magnificent. Thanks to the humid heat, his tanned, taut skin glistened. He combed a hand through his hair, and she could practically feel the softness in her own palm. As he walked forward, the muscles of his thighs and hips stretched and tightened, stealing her breath in a silent gasp. From the depth of his gaze to the hardness of his erection, it was clear the Adam Brody who stalked out onto the green was ready to seduce and be seduced. She bit her lip, grinned, then tore off her T-shirt, more than prepared to play her part.

"Sydney?"

By her nature, Sydney possessed a wealth of self-confidence about her intelligence and her savvy. Security about her body took a little more work. Hours jogging. Excessive time and cash spent on a personal trainer. Luckily for her, she liked to sweat, liked to push her muscles to the limit, liked to see the result of her hard work in the eyes of her lovers. Adam was no exception. Whenever he'd looked at her, she'd known he wanted her. Back at the cabin. In the car. At her condo.

And now. Nude in the moonlight, he wanted her. And she wanted him.

So simple, and yet she stopped in the shadows, wondering for a halting moment if making love with him now would help or hurt her ultimate goal—establishing a relationship with Adam that went deeper than sex, beyond physical pleasure. She'd recreated their last lovemaking session on the golf course in part to jog his memory, but also to reintroduce him to the fun, fancy-free tone of their past. But did she really want that? Was that really the way to go?

God, she didn't know. Not with any degree of certainty. She was taking a risk, bowing to her own needs. Her romance novels often depended on the thrill of the chase, the power of anticipation, an unpredictable route to love between the main characters. She'd been nicknamed Slow Burn Colburn for the trademark tease in her books, how she'd make her lovers wait to taste the fruit of their desires.

Sex meant conflict. Sex meant jumping into emotional quagmires where hearts sometimes got trampled or broken. Maybe that's why she'd simplified her own love life in the real world, so that the act meant nothing more than complete physical pleasure. No issues, no problems, no angst.

Yet with Adam, she'd discovered a new anticipation, a new type of chase. The challenge of elevating the sex they shared to a higher significance motivated her this time. Not knowing how the adventure would turn out spiked her passion to a level, so intense, she could hardly breathe.

She answered Adam's second call by emerging from the shadows. She walked slowly, enjoying the bounce of her breasts as she strolled up the hill, savoring the darkening of Adam's eyes and the tightening of his torso. He was hard, ready. And just thinking about feeling him inside her made her wet.

But not as wet as she would be in about sixty seconds.

"Where'd you go?" he asked.

"To set the mood. I wanted to recreate the last time we came here as accurately as possible."

When they were about five feet apart, she held her ground, content to study him from a distance for a moment, build the desire in visual degrees.

He'd never been so physically fit. So well muscled. He'd been a workout devotee, just like her. But now his exercise came from hard work. Outside. In the sweltering heat. She shivered, anticipating the scratch of his rough calluses on her tender skin.

"Sydney, I don't want you to be disappointed if I still don't remember us, even after tonight. The odds are against me, you know that, right?"

The night heat and Adam's proximity spawned a moist sheen over her skin, particularly beneath her hair. Sydney lifted the weight off her shoulders, well aware of how provocative the move would be. "My level of disappointment depends on what you do, Adam. Not on what you remember."

She walked closer, sidestepping a straight route, circling him so she could feast on every inch of his bare, naked body.

"Besides, your memory is having less and less to do with why we're here."

She watched his gaze sweep over her, the eyes of a hungry man. She doubted he could surpass her insatiable need, but she'd give him every opportunity to try.

He turned as she circled, his hands on his hips. "Really? Care to clue me in on the why else you brought me here?"

"You really need me to say it?"

"Not when you can show me."

"I will, Adam. In about thirty seconds."

They waited in silence, the distance between them crackling with sexual electricity. A shimmy of excitement trilled through her, the perfect prelude to the coming of the mist. Adam jumped forward when the sprinklers kicked on, grabbing her elbow to yank her toward the car, safely tucked in the trees.

She resisted, laughing. "No! This is how it was before!"

"We made love in the sprinklers?"

"Actually, it was raining. This was the best I could do."

He swept her into his arms, his chest rumbling and warm with humor. "Someone's going to call the groundskeeper. We're busted."

Sydney had considered that, but decided the payoff would be worth the risk. "That's why I called Chad before we left my place. He'll tell them he's on the problem, but he'll leave us alone. No one messes with his sprinkler system."

"You've thought of everything, haven't you?"

He pulled her flush against him, his eyes brimming with that halting intensity that truly made him the man she remembered. Powerful, passionate, proud.

She slipped her hands around his neck and pulled her lips to his, the swoosh and whir of the sprinklers drowning out her desperate moan.

"Did you get the condom?" she asked, kissing a path from his chin to his ear.

He flipped the foil packet from inside his palm. "Right here."

"Then, yes, I've thought of everything."

The sprinklers shot at them from three different directions, bathing them in cold droplets that contrasted with the heat all around them, inside them. After a few moments, they stopped yelping and laughing every time a splash coated their bodies with cool water. Adam took Sydney's hand and led her to a swell on the green that would hide them from the fairway, where he'd spread the old woolen blanket he must have found in her trunk. He knelt on the ground, then coaxed her beside him with a tug on her hand.

Knees touching, they faced each other. Adam released her hands and pressed them against her sides.

"Don't move for a minute."

"Why not?"

"That includes talking. I just want to look at you. Drink you in, so to speak."

"Drinking requires the use of your mouth," she teased.

He placed his index finger over her lips, silencing her. "Oh, I intend to use my mouth on you, Sydney.

And I intend to quench my thirst in lots of interesting ways. But first, stay still. I want to learn you, all over again."

ADAM WATCHED Sydney's eyes widen, then she smiled and dutifully took a deep breath, closed her eyes and lifted her chin just enough to tell him she anticipated this exploration the same way she looked forward to everything in her life. With great expectations. And no fear. And, ultimately, no regret. The way he wanted to live his life—and had—until the accident. Until he succumbed to the easy route and accepted his prescribed fate, rather than rewriting history the way he had once wanted to.

Well, now he had his second chance.

Sydney had to be the most fascinating part of the history he'd forgotten. When the sprinklers fanned another wave of rain over them, he watched her face tilt into the spray. Rivulets danced over her lashes and dripped down her cheeks, her neck, her breasts. Tiny droplets clung to her hard nipples, adding sparkles of light to her tanned skin, duskier in the puckered circles of her areola. His mouth dried, desperate to take the sweet moisture into his mouth—and he would, as soon as he looked his fill.

Water splashed down her torso, across her slim belly, over curved hips, then disappeared into the sweet triangle of curls at the apex of her thighs. She moved once, but only to push her increasingly saturated hair away from her face.

"You're beautiful," he said. "I wish I could say something more poetic, but—"

She shook her head, her mouth curved in a tiny smile, her neck arched, inviting. "I don't need poetry, Adam."

"You deserve poetry," he countered, wondering if he had the capacity to form musical, soulful words before the accident.

She snapped to face him. "Poetry is just words, Adam. Anybody can say words. Actions, now there's where a man makes his mark."

He formed tight fists, revving like a car stuck in Park while the driver tests the RPMs, wanting to touch her, but cursing that he had only two hands. Only ten fingers. Two lips. One tongue.

As if she sensed the tension, Sydney softly grasped his hands in hers and kneaded apart his rigid fingers, massaged his taut palms, placing a gentle kiss in the center of each hand. She looked down, carefully placing his hands on her body—one between her breasts where her heart pounded wildly, the other on her belly, where he felt a telltale quiver flutter across her skin.

"I've got you started," she said, her voice ragged, unsteady.

"Any preferences I should know about?" he asked, half teasing, half wondering just how Sydney liked her loving. From her bad-girl attitude and admittedly checkered past, he would have guessed their first love-making since their reunion would have been back in the parking garage up against the column in a rush of mindless lust, or maybe a gymnastic joining in the bucket seats of her Corvette. But the setting she'd chosen, tantilizing and forbidden, still held a sweet touch he found surprising. Even before the accident, he doubted he possessed the mindset to orchestrate something so sexy, yet so quixotic. As he slipped his hands over her wet skin, eliciting a sweet moan from her barely parted lips, he let the past go. There was only here, only now.

"Just touch me, Adam."

"That's my plan," he murmured. "Now lie back and enjoy. I'm going to take my time."

"But I want to touch you, too. We don't have to work one at a time. I don't know if I can wait."

No, but making her wait might keep him from going wild too soon. "I'll make it worth your while," he promised.

She leaned back to recline on the blanket, her hands cushioning her head, and she closed her eyes. "There you go with all those words again. Actions, Adam, actions."

He started with a kiss, loving her mouth completely. Her neck a graceful arch of sensitized flesh and pulse, proved just as tasty, just as susceptible to his tiny nips and licks. Against his chest, her nipples taunted him— tight and hard, brushing against his pecs, stirring his lust to near madness. He cupped her breasts, measuring, pleasuring, teasing the centers with his thumb until she cooed.

When he lowered his mouth for a taste, her hips bucked beneath his, seeking the hard heat of his erection. He moved until he nestled his sex between her thighs and she immediately rewarded him with a strangled cry.

The sprinklers soaked another layer of water over

them, blanketing them in wetness. He followed a straight path down from her breasts and when he took her with his mouth, he knew no sweeter heaven.

She came quickly, thoroughly, deeply. He caught the wave of her climax, urging her higher, faster, harder. Never once did she pull away from him, never once did she ask for mercy from the orgasmic explosions. Tasting her, hearing her, feeling her jump into the depths so freely nearly drove him insane.

He sat up and donned the condom, then stroked her thighs softly with his fingers until he sensed she'd returned to the world of the aware. She reached out with both hands and drew him over her.

"Inside, Adam."

"You don't have to ask twice."

"Good, because I never ask twice."

She was slick and warm and welcoming. She threaded her fingers through his hair and loved his neck and chest with long wet kisses that spiked his desire. In what seemed like a few seconds, his whole body surged with basic want. He could no longer contain his need. He entered her with all his power—and no control.

"Yes, Sydney. Oh, yes."

She met his rhythm, matched his heat. He grabbed her hands, twining their fingers as she lifted her knees, then wrapped her legs around his waist to lure him even deeper. The sensation toppled him until he burst into her, her name on his lips.

But he retained enough consciousness to realize she was still hot, still ready for more. He shifted his weight to one side to slip his hand between their slick, wet bodies. One touch, and she flew again into the rainbow abyss of sexual satisfaction.

Only when the sprinklers made one last pass over them and then shut off did they start to laugh. First a giggle, then a chuckle, then out and out mirth that forced an image of them running naked across the ninth hole into Adam's mind. He didn't dare voice his fantasy—he knew Sydney would have no compunction about taking off across the green, no matter who saw, no matter who knew. Not that he feared discovery in the least. He could think of no greater lark than streaking with Sydney. But if he wanted to make love to her again—which he did—he figured he'd best keep them out of a jail cell.

Despite the heat of the night, they soon began to shiver.

"I have no idea where my clothes are," Sydney said.

"Is there a law against driving home naked?"

"In a convertible? Definitely."

"And you know this...why?"

"I plead the fifth."

"We could put the top up," he suggested, knowing that while she may have misplaced her outfit, he knew where his pants and shirt were—in the front seat of the car. They could share. The thought of her petite body snuggled in his T-shirt held incredible appeal.

"Or we could just stay here forever," she answered dreamily.

"I'll bet tomorrow's first foursome would love it."

She skittered across the lawn and plucked her T-shirt off the ground, using the tiny white scrap of material to unsuccessfully wipe bits of grass off her body. They'd need another shower, though, this time, Adam hoped she'd opt for the type in a tile stall with a steady stream of hot water.

She lifted her eyebrow skeptically. "I'm not done with tonight. Are you?"

Done with tonight? Not a chance. Adam nearly tackled her, chasing her across the small hill and then scooping her into his arms. Her skin felt wet and cool against his, but he knew the heat she could generate from the inside. He wanted her again. Soon.

Then her expression grew serious, her emerald eyes intense. "Did you...?"

"Remember anything? Sydney, honey, you hardly gave me time to do *any* thinking."

His attempt to deflect her question with humor didn't work. Her mouth curved into a tiny frown, one he felt inexplicably compelled to kiss.

She turned her face, keeping him from distracting her. "No flashes of memory? No snippets of the past?"

"I was in the moment, Sydney. I hope you'll forgive me, but you only have yourself to blame."

She slapped his shoulder playfully, relaxing in his arms. "Sure, blame the woman. Isn't that always the way?"

SYDNEY COULDN'T REMEMBER the last time a man's laughter warmed her so thoroughly. Adam had always been an adventurous and carefree lover, but she still sensed a difference in him. A good one. He'd always laughed with her, teased her, quipped back with equal wit to whatever barb she'd thrown his way. But in contrast to the past, she knew now that the humor truly reached his heart, perhaps even his soul.

As he tossed her soiled T-shirt into the trunk with the sopping wet blanket, then pulled his T-shirt over her head like a parent dressing a child, she realized she didn't much care about the old Adam anymore. So the new Adam didn't remember her or making love in the rain that night on the golf course last year. So what? They had a new memory—a memory that existed for both of them.

He shrugged into his jeans as best as a wet man could. "I'll drive."

She smiled and slid into the passenger seat. "Do you know the way back?" After buckling her seat belt, she snuggled sideways onto the seat, her legs tucked beneath her. She closed her eyes, and felt a small but incredibly satisfied smile on her lips.

"Funny how the road leading to your bedroom seems clear as a bell."

She hummed, lulled by the revving engine and Adam's nearness into a twilight sleep. Exhausted, she needed a catnap to revitalize her body. Clear her mind.

They had a long night ahead of them and Sydney wanted to savor every single second.

9

BY THE TIME THEY RETURNED to Sydney's condo, exhaustion won out over desire. They showered, then fell into bed, sleeping soundly, Sydney curled up with her hand beneath her pillow, Adam spooned beside her with his arm across her belly. Only when she got up around 3:00 a.m. to go to the bathroom and get a drink of water from the kitchen did she notice the red light blinking on her answering machine. She had an unlisted number, so whoever had left the message was likely someone she knew.

She checked the caller ID, which came through blank. Odd. She had an intercept system to avoid unsolicited calls. Lowering the volume, she pressed the button, both hoping and dreading that the call, which had come just past midnight, was from Jillian, the only person she knew who could bypass the telephone company.

Sydney grinned when she heard her new friend's voice. The private investigator was not only good, she was diligent. Sydney rubbed the sleep from her eyes, flipped on the kitchen light, and replayed the message, this time jotting down the important details on a small legal pad she kept near the phone.

"Who was that?"

Adam crossed the threshold wearing nothing but a

towel around his waist and a tired smile. A thrill fluttered deep in her belly, and Sydney had to sit down before the shaking weakened her knees. She hadn't reacted to the fact that he was devastatingly handsome and immeasurably sexy. He *was,* of course, but that hadn't rocked her equilibrium. The minute he'd stepped into her kitchen, she'd experienced a homey, comfortable warmth unlike anything she'd ever felt before.

Oh, God. She was in deep.

"Jillian. She called while we were out."

Interest shined in his eyes, but he crossed to the cupboard, searched for a glass, then poured himself water from the dispenser in the door of the fridge. "She found something already?"

"I told you, she's the best."

Sydney reached over to the counter and replayed the message for Adam, holding up the pad of paper so he knew she'd written the information down.

Jillian's voice sounded sleepy, but excited. "Hey, Sydney. Here's what I've got so far. Kyle Sanderson. 1445 Shore Side Boulevard, Apartment 2-A. Current employment, Sanderson Investments, which operates mostly in day trading. Same address." She rattled off Kyle's phone numbers, including his unlisted private line and his cell phone. Jillian also provided her with the name and address of the guy's current girlfriend, his mother's phone number and address in Palm Harbor and the make, model, year and license number of his car. "I'll be waiting to hear from you. Let me know what, if anything, you want me to do next."

"Bayshore, huh? Was he from money?" Adam asked.

Sydney shook her head. "I suppose it's possible. He sure didn't act rich. Maybe he just did a prodigal son thing. But if his family was rich, he never mentioned it to me."

"Not that you would have asked."

She frowned at him. "No, I wouldn't have asked. Personal disclosure, particularly about finances, is entirely voluntary. But I do know he couldn't have afforded that pricey address when I knew him."

Adam's lips drew into a straight line while he mulled over the information. Interesting information. Information that made Sydney's creative mind work overtime with nefarious possibilities that chilled her blood midstream.

Her onetime overnight courier now owned and operated an investment firm—in South Tampa, an area known mainly for old money, but increasingly more for the new. She wondered how much capital someone would need for such a venture. How much education. Kyle hadn't struck her as particularly savvy or full of untapped potential. Then again, she never would have pegged him as a thief, either.

She checked the address again, and realized he didn't live in an apartment, but in a condominium complex overlooking Tampa Bay. "This address is more than just old money," she told him.

She scooted the pad across the table so he could take a look.

"It's one of Tampa's few bayfront condo properties.

I follow real estate," she explained, noting his questioning look.

"More expensive than this place?"

"Most definitely. Kyle has moved up." She told him how when she and Kyle had had their fling, they'd met only at her place. And if her memory served, Kyle had told her at the time that he lived in the University of South Florida area, somewhere near the financially unstable "Suitcase City" neighborhood.

"To go from the dregs to the old-monied part of town takes one thing and one thing only," Adam concluded. "Money. And lots of it."

She tapped her fingers on the table, nodding in agreement.

"So where did the windfall come from?" Adam asked, his tone rhetorical.

Still, Sydney couldn't help the first answer that popped into her head, though she managed enough sensitivity to keep it to herself.

A payoff.

Sometimes being a writer sucked. Sydney could no more look at a situation and see the innocent possibilities first than she could visit a new, exciting place and not immediately consider how she could work it into a book. From the moment she first set pen to paper at age six, she viewed the world in terms of subplots and conflicts and ulterior motives. When you wrote about them often enough, they became part of your everyday world. It did a real number on her ability to trust.

Inheritance or hard work didn't ring true as explanations for Kyle's new wealth. He'd made the money the fast and easy way—the illegal way. And, possibly, at the price of Adam's life.

Sydney considered brewing a pot of coffee and discussing their next step in the dim light of the kitchen, then decided she'd rather they talk in the comfort of her bed. With his arms around her, she figured they could solve the world's problems in about twenty minutes, then could move on to matters more interesting.

"Let's go back to bed."

"I'm not sure I can sleep," Adam said, his tone brimming with seriousness, his gaze locked on the legal pad in front of her, too far away for him to make out the scribbles.

"That's okay by me."

She flipped the paper over, then slinked across the kitchen in her sexiest sashay. "There's nothing we can do to investigate Kyle tonight. We know where he lives, where he works, where he hangs out. I'm sure Jillian hasn't done anything during her investigation to tip Kyle off that we're looking for him and checking into his current situation."

Adam's scowl lost some of its shadow. "Well," he conceded, "if he's stayed in town all this time, he must consider himself safe from anyone connecting him to my missing plans."

She slipped her hands around his waist, then placed a butterfly kiss on his hard pec. "So he'll stay put until tomorrow, right? Let's go make the best of what's left of the night."

His chest hair tickled her nose, so she lowered her mouth to his smooth nipple.

"Sydney, I need to think about this."

"What's to think about now that can't be thought about tomorrow? Kyle has a lot of money, money he may have gotten as a payoff for swiping your plans, like you said. But I'll bet the entire worth of his new digs that we won't find out for sure until we pay him a little visit."

"'We'?"

"Yes, 'we,' as in you and me. We've been working on 'we' all night, Adam. Where the heck have you been?"

He snagged her around the waist, pulling her flush against his body. In an instant, the sash to her robe and his towel lay in a tangled mess on the floor.

"Right here with you, Colburn."

"You're planning to check him out, aren't you?"

Adam grinned. "Of course. I doubt he'll admit anything to me, but I want to see his reaction when he realizes I'm alive and looking for him."

Sydney snuggled closer, glad they were on the same page. "Good. Then we're thinking alike."

"Not exactly. I don't think you should come with me tomorrow. Thanks to you, I have a name and an address. I can check things out on my own."

"You can," Sydney said reasonably, "but you won't."

"I won't?"

"Why would you? I'm your best weapon to shake the guy up. Kyle must know I'm the one person who remembers seeing him take the plans."

It only took a split second for Adam's face to lose all semblance of humor. Sydney replayed what she'd said, then realized the inherent danger—that is, if she considered Kyle dangerous, which she didn't. She was the only witness to a crime that might have precipitated a near-fatal hit-and-run.

"You're not going," he said, his tone clear and final.

Sydney tried not to bristle, but thirty-something years of independent living made the task impossible. "The hell I'm not," she protested, pulling out of his embrace. "Look, I understand the danger. But I'm your ace in the hole. My presence could spook Kyle enough for him to reveal some fact he isn't supposed to reveal."

"How do you know he wasn't the one who tried to kill me, too?"

"Because he would have come after me to keep me from connecting him to the crime. Look, I may take lovers the same way some women choose tomatoes at the market, but I'm not entirely indiscriminate. Kyle always struck me as a gentle soul. Not too bright, but a kind heart."

Of course, she could be wrong. But it didn't happen often, so she tossed that possibility aside. She appreciated Adam's protective streak, but she wasn't going to let a little potential trouble deter her. He'd already been hit by a car and left for dead. Lost his business and his career. Been hurt on so many levels that night a year ago—and she hadn't been there to help, hadn't even known. If he ran afoul of some wicked plot again, the least she could do was run interference.

"You need my help, Adam," she insisted. "Get used to the idea."

He opened his mouth, his gaze afire, then he stopped and pulled her back into his arms. "Sydney, I couldn't handle something happening to you. If you can finger him for a crime, he might still hurt you to keep you quiet."

She snuggled closer, satisfied at least that her nearness caused his body to harden and heat. She wasn't beyond using sex to convince him, but she preferred good old-fashioned logic. Its persuasive power had a longer-lasting effect.

"If he thought I was going to squeal, wouldn't he have done something about me by now? I haven't gotten so much as an ill-timed visit or threatening letter in the past year. Even my you-write-porno-trash hate mail has been at an all-time low."

"Maybe that's just because you went out of town right afterward. Maybe he figures that you never saw me again, never put two-and-two together. Now that we're..."

His voice trailed off as he lost the words to explain the current state of their relationship. She considered what he might say, then realized what they'd established tonight was hard to define. Yes, they were lovers again. But not like they had been in the past, where the *f* word best described the emotional depth of what they'd shared. Now things were different. Deeper. More significant.

Like friendship.

"No one knows we're seeing each other again, except for Renée and Jillian. No one else has to know," she said. "But I'm your best bet in getting Kyle to spill. I don't think he did this on his own, but he might have done it for someone else. He's more likely to screw up around me than he is with you."

Adam's face turned to stone, but when she popped a kiss onto the tip of his nose, followed by a swipe of a lick across his lips, his facade broke into a resigned smile.

"I'm not letting you confront him by yourself. That's out of the question." He pointed his finger for emphasis. His chest grew rigid, his voice stern.

He was darned adorable when he was all manly and protective. "Okay."

"What? That was too easy."

"You're a very convincing man. I promise that I won't confront him on my own."

He remained silent for a minute, and she could feel his shocked stare boring through the top of her head. She stifled a chuckle.

"We'll work together," he clarified.

"Absolutely."

She nibbled her way up to his mouth and then flung off her robe the minute his tongue met hers. Passion exploded with instantaneous fire and within minutes he was carrying her toward the staircase.

Only after he laid her down on the bed, then proceeded to kiss a trail from her toes on up, did Sydney allow herself a triumphant smile. If they both worked on the case, they'd have to spend lots of time together—a very attractive plan if she did say so herself.

SOMETIME AROUND DAWN, Adam awoke and stifled a chuckle. Minx. She'd manipulated him with no more effort than it took one of Renée's cats to catch a lizard on the back porch. He distinctly remembered wanting to meet this Kyle Sanderson alone, without dragging Sydney into a situation that might be dangerous. People involved in crimes that garnered valuable stolen property tended to be antsy, unpredictable. The accident that had nearly killed him might not have been an accident at all. Those architectural plans had been worth millions to him and to contractors interested in revolutionizing the design of office buildings. But had Kyle Sanderson known that? Chances were the guy was just a pawn—manipulated because of his courier job and access to Adam's plans. But Adam couldn't be sure without probing further. Thanks to Jillian, and with Sydney's help, he was closer to finding out the truth. And with a few details from his former assistant, he'd know precisely how to proceed with Kyle.

At 6:00 a.m., he snuck out of bed and called Renée from Sydney's kitchen, knowing his sister had kept in touch with Meg. An early riser, Renée sounded anxious when she answered the phone.

"You okay?" she asked.

"I'm great. Can we leave it at that?"

"Absolutely," Renée answered. "I don't want to pry in your love life."

Adam laughed. "Yeah, right. You don't want to pry because you don't need to. You know what's happening between Sydney and me."

"Are you calling me at six o'clock in the morning to rub it in my face that you have a love life and I don't?"

Renée was joking, with no underlying regret apparent in her voice. Still, now that he'd experienced a delicious taste of reconnecting with Sydney, he wondered if his sister didn't need a jolt to her social life. Someone to throw a wrench in her safe, predictable world. Someone who'd make her want to take risks again, just as Sydney had with him.

Well, that was a conversation for another time and place. He'd worry about Renée's love life—or lack thereof—when he didn't have so much on his own personal plate. Following new leads. Tracking down his stolen plans. Figuring out why Sydney no longer felt like a stranger to him after one short night, even though he hadn't remembered a single thing about her or their past relationship.

Yup. His plate runneth over.

"I'm calling because I need Meg's number."

Silence crackled over the connection. "Why?"

"I need to ask her about the courier."

"I thought Sydney knew the courier. I thought she was going to help you find him."

"She is, but I need to know if the same courier ever picked up from my office, if he had any way of knowing how valuable the plans were."

"Did you find the guy already?"

Adam realized his sister was avoiding his question and cursed himself for not just calling Information for Meg's number. But he had promised to update Renée, and this call could achieve two goals if she'd simply co-operate.

"We're close. We have an address."

"Have you called the police?"

Adam didn't need to explain this again to his sister. "It's six o'clock in the morning, Renée. Please, just give me her number."

"Hold on."

After a few minutes, she returned to the phone, rattled off Meg's number and new work schedule, then gave him the name and phone number of the detective who had worked his case. Adam barely remembered the man since his last interview had been while he was still in rehab, but he did recall the policeman's frustration at not truly being able to help Adam. He carefully read back the two numbers to Renée to ensure he got them right. With a situation so important, he wasn't ruling out any avenue of assistance.

"Call me later?" Renée requested, her voice smaller and quaking with an emotion Adam instantly recognized as genuine worry.

"Absolutely. Look, while I'm running around trying to settle this, why don't you take a few days off? You're caught up on orders. Wasn't your friend Betty going down to her mom's beach place this week?"

Renée's hesitation told him she was truly considering his suggestion. While his baby sister had devoted herself to his recovery over the past year, she did have good friends who shanghaied her out of the house every so often for pizza, a movie, or just a beer at a nearby roadhouse. She didn't shun social interaction so much as she just forgot about it until a friend—or her brother—reminded her.

"I don't want to be away from the phone," she answered. "What if you need me, like now?"

"You've got the cell—take it with you. It's one day, Renée. Have a little fun while I'm gone."

He heard his sister's deep-throated chuckle, a sound that often alleviated the guilt he associated with her devotion to his care. "What the hell. You're having a little fun, right?"

"I'm having *a lot* of fun, but you didn't want me to go there."

"Right, thanks for reminding me. I'll take the cell, but you promise to call me tonight."

"I promise."

He hung up, then jogged back up the stairs. Surrounded by no less than seven pillows—one particularly fluffy one smashed over her face so that only her mouth and nose were visible—Sydney looked the ultimate modern lady of leisure, used to living alone, comfortable with her nudity, accustomed to hogging the blanket that covered all of her except one breast.

A breast his mouth watered to taste. His sex stiffened. All thoughts not related to making love to Sydney flew out of his brain. He took one step toward her, then stopped and stuffed all those errant thoughts back inside.

For the past year, Adam had tried not to think about regaining all he'd lost since the accident—tried not to hope that the dead ends the police encountered in their investigations might miraculously open up and point to a path to justice. Nothing so drastic had happened yet, but thanks to Sydney he at least had a place to start.

But where would his quest leave her?

She'd told him yesterday that she needed to reassess what she wanted from him since learning about his accident. She'd originally wanted to rekindle what had almost been a serious relationship. After spending one electric night with her, he couldn't blame her. They were amazing together, like a hammer and nail in the hands of a master craftsman. Their rhythms matched, their mutual chemistry blended into a potentially explosive elixir that might blast him free from all the pain of his past.

Only, that was the problem, wasn't it. Despite his amnesia, Adam didn't want to forget his past. Sure, he'd tried not to dwell there since his recovery, but the hunger to find out the truth, the thirst to retrieve what he'd worked so hard to create, never completely ceased. Sydney symbolized two things—his key to unlocking the mystery behind his accident and a chance at an exciting future. But as far as he was concerned, he couldn't have the future he wanted without first putting his past to rest.

So, for today, he'd focus on the present. Here. Now. In bed, with Sydney. He grinned stupidly for a minute, then a blast from the air conditioner reminded him that he had no good reason to look at her from a distance when he could snuggle beside her instead.

"Your feet are cold," she mumbled, then yawned, remembering to cover her mouth at the very last second.

"So are yours." He tweaked her erect nipple. "Your breasts are a bit icy, too. But don't worry, I'll warm them up."

"What about my feet?"

He tossed aside the pillow covering her face, then straddled her. "We'll get to your feet," he promised. "How 'bout I start at the top and work my way down?"

"YOU'RE ALL SET," Jillian announced, turning toward her desk and clipping her briefcase closed. They'd spent the last fifteen minutes attaching a minuscule microphone to Sydney's right breast, the same breast Adam had suckled for a dizzying amount of time that morning, so that Sydney's body still thrummed with the memory. The tape itched a little on her sensitive skin, but as she adjusted her blouse and glanced in the mirror, she understood why Jillian got paid the big bucks. Even in Sydney's sexy attire—meant to shake Kyle Sanderson up enough to make him let something slip about the night of Adam's accident—no one would ever guess she was wearing a wire.

"You do good work," Sydney complimented, unzipping her skirt so she could tuck her blouse back inside her waistband.

"Yes, I do," Jillian replied, slipping a sharp gray suit jacket over a pearl blouse, looking a tad too formal for her casual personality. "Sure you don't want to put this operation off until this afternoon? I'll be done with my appointment by two o'clock. I could ride backup."

Sydney shook her head, then nodded toward the door. Adam waited in the hallway. If not for the fact that Jillian assured her the walls were reinforced to contain private conversations, Sydney might not have been so forthcoming.

"Adam wants to do this, Jillian. He wasn't so happy about me helping him at first. Luckily, he yielded to my powers of persuasion."

Jillian winked. "Typical male."

Sydney wanted to agree, but found herself shaking her head instead. "You know, he's anything but typical. A woman could fall hard for a man like him."

Jillian's grin bloomed. "Sydney Colburn! You're totally ruining the reputation that precedes you."

Sydney would have asked "what reputation?" but she knew perfectly well what Jillian meant. The two women only knew each other because Jillian's husband, Cade Lawrence, a former cop, had once been partners with Jake Tanner, who had married Sydney's best friend, Devon. The ladies had played poker once and had chatted at Devon's bridal shower and bachelorette party. Though she hadn't known what Jillian did for a living until Cassie told her, the two women had immediately taken a liking to one another. And with Devon on her honeymoon, Sydney was glad to have a friend she could trust, particularly one with such awesome investigative skills.

"I'm still the same woman," Sydney insisted. "It's just that he's a different guy."

"Different from who he was before his accident or different from any other man you've met?"

Sydney bit her bottom lip. She hadn't been back with Adam long enough to pinpoint or analyze what she felt for him or even specifically how he'd changed. She only knew that the man she'd considered strong as a titan now surpassed even that bold description. The man she'd considered brave and driven and sharp now gave her new definitions for all those words. He was new and improved, and yet gentler than before—cautious, not because of fear, but because he cared. Because he knew the value of life.

"Both," she finally answered.

"Girl, you're in big trouble."

"Tell me about it. But it's nothing I didn't ask for." She adjusted her blouse to achieve maximum cleavage. She'd foolishly thought she could seduce Adam into remembering her, but she'd blown that one. Undaunted, this time she'd go for seducing him into falling in love. Simple, right?

"And nothing I can't handle," she finished.

"That, I do not doubt."

Jillian opened the door to her office and waved Adam inside. While Jillian briefed him on the simple operation of the listening device, Sydney eased onto the couch in Jillian's office and pretended to adjust the straps on her high heels. She tilted her leg sideways, toying with the tiny buckle, certain Adam could glimpse the lacy top of her thigh-high hose. She'd worn panties, but they were of the thong variety, so they didn't offer much coverage. When he bobbled the keys Jillian tossed across her desk, he bent to retrieve them and she was certain he'd cast a long glance her way.

"Take my car," Jillian instructed. "You can monitor

the conversations between Kyle and Sydney from the receiver built into my radio."

Adam pocketed the keys with way more finesse than he'd caught them, giving Sydney a chastising look. "You women sure play fast and furious with your vehicles."

"We have no emotional attachment to rubber and steel like you men do," Jillian answered, snagging her briefcase and hustling them toward the door.

"Speak for yourself," Sydney countered. "I love my Corvette. I've been told my attachment has something to do with my childhood."

Jillian laughed as she led them through the maze of security codes and automatic locks that was the Hennessy Group offices. "I'll need the Mustang back by two. Let me see the keys again?"

Adam produced them from his pocket.

"Click this—" Jillian indicated the button on the remote key entry device "—to disengage the alarm. Once you're inside, slide this—" she jangled the keychain to draw his attention to a fuzzy green teddy bear dangling on the ring "—over the silver plate just under the steering wheel."

"Does the car blow up if I don't?" Adam asked.

Jillian patted his arm assuringly. "Nothing so dramatic. You'll just get zapped with about fifty volts of electricity from the steering wheel. And the car won't start. I think the doors automatically lock, too, but I don't remember. It's not a feature I use regularly."

"You've got to love modern technology," he said.

"Woe to the teenager who decides to heist your car for a joyride," Sydney added, shaking her head.

"Yeah, well, I like feeling safe about things," Jillian answered. "Wish I could say I feel safe about you two trying to pull a fast one on Kyle Sanderson. He may seem harmless, Sydney, but you never know what someone is willing to do for money," she warned.

Sydney shook her head, determined not to let Jillian spook her. She'd spent all morning reminding Adam that she had the best shot at extracting information from Kyle and convincing herself that, while she wasn't invincible by any means, she was fast on her feet and fairly resourceful. Thanks to Jillian's wiretap, Adam would be only a whisper away. And she owed him this risk.

She wasn't sure why she owed him yet, but she knew deep in her heart that she did. He'd lost more in one night than she had in her entire life. Besides, she cared about him deeply. She had before, but hadn't had the courage to admit it. Instead, she'd walked away. And Sydney hated being redundant, particularly when the repetition included making the same mistake twice.

"I realize that. But what Kyle might have done for money is nothing compared to what I'm willing to do for great sex."

10

FROM THE LOOK on Kyle's face, Sydney had chosen her outfit well—from her low-cut gold silk blouse designed to emphasize her breasts, to the teardrop emerald pendant nestled at the deepest juncture of her cleavage, to her sinfully short skirt. She'd paired the breezy blouse with black—black supersheer hose, and a sleek black cotton-blend skirt. She'd bypassed leather—some things were overkill. And while Sydney intended to play this game for the ultimate win, she would do so with finesse.

Adam was, after all, listening. Knowing he could hear the sound of her heartbeat from the tiny microphone Jillian had taped beneath her bra added a sexual undertone to the entirely serious affair. And since Adam insisted he handle the surveillance on his own, Sydney could say whatever she wanted without anyone but him hearing.

An idea clicked in her mind, but she filed it away for after she'd finished this business with Kyle. She had rung the bell of his swanky South Tampa townhome, then stepped back from the polished oak door and struck a sexy pose, in case he peeked out the peephole. Information now, games later. Not her usual mode of operation, but, hey, she could adapt.

Kyle had answered quickly. "Sydney! What are you doing here?"

She grinned slyly and grabbed the doorjamb. Just when she saw him relax in the belief that she was content to remain outside and chat, she swung past him and marched through the foyer. She'd no plans to wait for a formal invitation inside. She had work to do.

The entryway took her past a formal dining room and gourmet kitchen, then opened onto a huge great room with a fourteen-foot cathedral ceiling. A bank of windows across the far end provided an impressive, unhampered view of the bay, with Tampa's growing skyline providing a cosmopolitan backdrop. Kyle's couch and chairs were leather, his end tables and coffee tables sculpted stone and topped with hand-etched glass.

"Wow," she said, turning a full circle to take in the rather esoteric, yet expensive, art gracing the walls. "You've certainly moved on up. If this were a high rise, I could sing the theme song to *The Jeffersons*."

Kyle made a sound that resembled a laugh. He shut the door and hurried toward her, as if he had somewhere he needed to go.

"My luck changed. Look, Sydney, I'd love to show you around, but I've got an appointment in twenty minutes. Do you think we could do this later maybe?"

She speared him with a disbelieving look. "You know me, Kyle. Now or never."

He watched her walk across the room, and slowly his eyes narrowed. "Why are you here, Sydney?"

Aha. Smart boy. She certainly wasn't here to jump into bed with him. No matter that making him believe she'd come here for sex might have helped her, Sydney decided she'd only go so far. "I just need a little information. Nothing too hard."

"Are you implying that I'm stupid?"

"I don't toy with stupid men, Kyle. You must be pretty darned smart to have amassed enough money to afford this place. I don't suppose you want to tell me how you did that?"

"What? You writing a book?"

She scoffed at his lame attempt at a joke. "Not presently."

"I saw you made the *New York Times* again."

His attempt to change the subject didn't deter her, but she did acknowledge that perhaps Kyle was a tad slicker than she remembered. That was okay by her. She could be slick, too. "That's why I'm here, in a roundabout sort of way."

Not a lie. Not the truth, but most definitely not a lie.

She slid down onto the leather couch, crossing her legs high at the thigh so he could catch a glimpse of her lace-topped hose. She'd performed the move on Adam just this morning, but the lecherous look on Kyle's face did nothing but make her force a smile.

He slung his hands in his pockets, a sure sign that she'd piqued more than just his intellectual interest. "What do I have to do with you making the *Times*?"

"I've been spending some time looking up some old friends from back when I was writing that book. You're one. Adam Brody is another."

She watched his face, caught the twitch in his jaw, the quick glance to the floor that spoke volumes. She may not have been trained as a private investigator, but as a writer Sydney had long made a habit of watching people, studying them, guessing the underlying meanings to their expressions and trying to stick around long enough to see if she was right.

Kyle didn't like that she'd mentioned Adam. He didn't like it one bit.

"Who?"

Lame-o. "Adam Brody. The architect? He used to have a condo across from mine."

This time he hid his emotions behind deep thought. "Oh, yeah. 8-B, right? Light brown hair? Tall?"

"About six foot two. Caramel hair. Could lose yourself in those almond eyes. Do you know what happened to him?"

Sydney didn't have to feign the wistful sound in her voice.

"You lost touch with him? Weren't you two involved?"

Sydney shrugged. "We went our separate ways. I went on a book tour a year ago and then on vacation. I was gone a long time and when I got back, he was gone. I tried looking him up, but struck out. Now I have something I need to return to him. Since I made the *Times*, I've decided to move to New York. Be closer to my publisher."

She and Adam had concocted this lie over breakfast in bed. They'd verified the idea with Jillian, who thought the ruse might work. The experienced investigator had worried a little over the inherent danger of confronting Kyle with too many questions, so they'd also discussed adding one more of Jillian's gadgets to the mix. Sydney clutched the tiny "bug" in her hand, waiting for a chance to plant it in Kyle's apartment so she and Adam could hear what might go down after she dropped her bomb and left.

"When do you leave?" he asked, his tone casual, but he'd licked his lips one time too many, a facial tic Sydney attributed to true nervousness.

"Tomorrow, actually. But I have these plans, blueprints, that Adam asked I take with me to Scotland, to keep safe. I don't know, I guess they're valuable. Anyway, I figured he'd contact me again after I got back, but I haven't heard a word. Since I knew you'd been at the condo that night, I wondered if maybe you had some idea of what happened to him."

"You remember that I was there?"

Small beads of sweat formed just over Kyle's thin upper lip, causing Sydney's heart to beat faster. She wondered if Adam could truly hear the pounding vibrate as hard against the microphone as it seemed to against her chest.

She attempted a nonchalant wave. "No big deal. It's not like I think you're unforgettable or anything." She used the saucy teasing as a prelude to stand. She wandered the room, picking up a brass statuette of an ibis and examining it closely. "But I did want to look you up, see what you've been up to and how you've been doing before I took off. Then I thought if you knew anything about Adam, I'd do the two-birds, one-stone thing. No biggie. I'll just toss the plans or something."

"Toss them?" He voice cracked up an octave, before he cleared his throat. "Don't you think they might be important?"

She wandered to the bookshelves and ran her fingernail over the perfect uncracked spines. Decorative, un-read books. What a waste of trees.

"I guess. But I checked with his sister. She and Adam don't get along," she lied, inserting this detail to ensure that Kyle or whoever paid him to filch the plans left Re-née alone, "but she said he sold his business, his place, everything and just took off. Sounded odd to me, but, hey, maybe he had an early midlife crisis or some-thing."

"Do you have the plans with you?"

Sydney arched a brow, but lowered it before she faced him. Odd question. She and Adam hadn't planned on using her as bait, so she knew the answer she was supposed to give Kyle, to throw him off track. For an instant, she considered defiance. Maybe the bait thing wasn't such a reckless idea. Yet the minute she considered rebellion and nearly told Kyle she did in-deed currently have the last known copy of the plans, she imagined Adam cursing her on the other side of her microphone for inviting danger. Part of her wanted him to sweat awhile, just for fun, but she certainly didn't want him charging up the stairs and ruining the whole operation.

"No, they're with my attorney. I'll just have him hang on to them. If I don't find Adam first, that is."

"You going to keep looking?"

Sydney pursed her lips, pretending the question re-quired great effort and thought. "I don't know. If the mood takes me. I've already given the guy more atten-tion than he deserves."

Ouch. She hated saying that, hated pretending that Adam wasn't back in her life, even if it was to force the hand of a transparent opportunist. Maybe she'd never recognized the streak in Kyle since he'd never wanted anything more from her than sex, which, at the time, she'd been willing to give. Now she knew he was nervous, knew her visit had thrown him off-kilter. But she wasn't done yet, and she certainly couldn't leave until she convinced him that her visit had been merely the execution of a whim.

She continued strolling around the room, admiring his knickknacks, asking him questions so he could brag about his new business, which he'd supposedly started thanks to the investment generosity of a friend. In the middle of his rather dry diatribe on the rise and fall of day trading, she found a spot near his phone to hide the small listening device. Unfortunately, his phone was portable. If he wandered, they might not hear much. But, if he was involved in the theft of Adam's plans, and acted in accordance with Jillian's instincts, he'd soon make a frantic phone call to whomever was behind the plot.

And he wouldn't have expected Sydney Colburn, devil-may-care romance novelist, to have planted a bug in his house so they could listen to his every word.

ADAM ADJUSTED the frequency on Jillian's radio the moment Sydney emerged from Kyle's townhouse. She glanced over her shoulder, and with no front window for Kyle to watch her through, apparently felt safe enough to dash across street to where he'd parked the Mustang under a thick, low-hanging tree. By the time she opened the passenger door and maneuvered her tight skirt and slim legs into the car, he'd found the sound of Kyle cursing.

"Guess he wasn't so glad to see me, huh?" Sydney asked.

"Can you blame him? You are a merciless tease."

"I think today is the first time anyone could actually call me a tease and get away with it."

Kyle's cursing quieted and they heard the clatter of him grabbing the phone.

"I wouldn't presume to call you anything. You've already given me more attention than I deserve, remember?"

She waved her hand at him. "You know that was just part of the act."

He suppressed a laugh, determined to use her comment as sensual leverage later on. "Fine. I'll let you make it up to me."

Her comment had muted the sound of whomever Kyle had asked for on the other line. He wanted to shush her, but figured doing so might cause him permanent physical damage.

Luckily, she'd heard and lowered her voice herself. "Oh, I'll make it up to you, all right."

At that, Adam reached across, took her hand and placed a sweep of kisses across her knuckles. "I'm looking forward to—"

"We've got a problem." Kyle's voice was strong at first, then started to fade.

"Phone's portable," Sydney said, frustrated.

Adam nodded. Jillian had warned him that they'd run into this problem lately with the standard under-the-table bug. But he hadn't wanted to wait until Jillian could arrange a more reliable one that attached to the innards of the phone or a radar device that required a big vanful of equipment and qualified personnel to operate.

"Sydney Colburn came to see me today." Pause. "Oh, yeah, I didn't ever tell you about her, did I. She was there the night I took the plans."

Well, at least they had their confession, inadmissible as it was. Adam had decided this morning that if the police needed useable evidence, then they could darn well get it themselves. Wiretap orders required time and a judge's signature—and he didn't have the patience to wait for the police to get either. He wanted his plans back, and he wanted them now. He'd already lost a year of his life. If he had a shot at speeding things up, he was going for it.

"Because she was a friend. I didn't want you going after her. It's been a year, and you've sold your plans to your foreigners. She hasn't caused us any trouble. She probably isn't any trouble now, except she told me that Brody gave her a copy of the plans for safekeeping. And he's never claimed them. She's looking for the dude now."

They listened a few more minutes, Adam's anger raging by degrees with each detail Kyle revealed. He had indeed taken a payoff to set up the fake courier pickup and had stolen the plans, though how he'd learned about the pickup order or that Adam had finished the plans was still an unknown. Kyle had been aware of Adam's accident, though, from the tone of the conversation, the former courier hadn't realized the hit-and-run was a setup until after the fact. Seemingly, his one job had been to steal the plans and for that he'd gotten enough cash to start his business.

He'd told Sydney that he had quadrupled the initial "investment" amount in less than a year. The nest egg now gave him a fearless attitude about his former— and still nameless—compatriot. He colorfully informed the person on the other end of the line that he didn't give a damn how the situation was handled so long as his part of the scheme was never exposed.

The fact that Kyle also seemed intent on protecting Sydney from whomever he'd conspired with kept Adam from marching upstairs right this minute and beating the identity of the other person on the line out of his skanky, opportunistic body. Kyle bought the lie that Sydney had left the plans with her attorney, making them essentially untouchable. He also related Sydney's untruth about Adam's falling out with Renée, and Adam's supposed disappearance into parts unknown.

"If he wanted those plans, he could have found her. I don't think you have to worry, except now there's proof that he designed that building."

A long pause ensued. They could hear a whiny drone, as if the person on the other end of the line was shouting. Kyle only laughed. "That's your problem. I did my part. Keep me out of it."

He disconnected the call, sending Sydney into overdrive, the last part of their predetermined plan. She jogged back to Kyle's front door, as best she could in her sexy high heels, and knocked.

Adam turned the radio back to the frequency that picked up the microphone taped beneath Sydney's blouse. He intended to find that wire very, very soon. He might just remove it with his teeth, like he had her panties the night before. She did owe him after that crack about giving him more attention than he deserved. And he knew just how he planned for her to pay. Luckily for him, he knew Sydney would be game.

"Hey, I'm sorry. My cell phone is out of power and I was supposed to call my stylist when I was on my way to the salon. Could I use your phone for a sec?"

Adam lifted his binoculars. Kyle looked flustered, but nodded. "Sure. If you promise to let me know where you're living when you get to New York. I've always wanted to go there. I could look you up."

"Sure, it'd be a kick."

For that, he'd make her do a striptease. He'd been thinking nonstop about those thigh-high hose with the lacy tops. He wanted to watch her roll each one down, slowly, revealing inch after inch of smooth, tanned leg. And the thong panties. Oh, he had definite suggestions for what to do with those.

He listened to Sydney go to the phone and punch in numbers. He heard her pretend to speak with Robert, her stylist. She did a great job of simulating chitchat, when he knew she was using the automatic call-back feature on the phone. When she hung up, she thanked Kyle and hightailed it out of there.

This time, Kyle lingered at the door, so Sydney went straight to where she'd parked the Corvette, got in and revved the engine. Only after she'd backed out of the space and turned onto the redbrick road leading out of the complex did Kyle disappear back inside.

Adam started the Mustang and followed, wondering what she'd learned. "Come on, Sydney. Speak to me."

But the wire she wore worked only in one direction. He followed her around downtown, then onto the expressway, listening with frustration as she played with the radio, found a song she liked, then proceeded to sing along.

He sped up behind her, but the Mustang, a borrowed one at that, was no match for the Corvette. She maneuvered her car around a slow-moving truck, then dashed off the exit by Jillian's office, putting at least four cars between them.

She lowered the volume of her radio and made tsk-tsk noises. "Bad boy, Adam. It's not nice to speed in someone else's car. You know the way back to Jillian's office. Park in the shade, in that corner away from the street."

Aha. He did as she asked, knowing she intended to start paying him back for that errant comment earlier. He scanned the quiet residential road that crossed in front of the office building. Though it was nearly one o'clock and employees on the way back from lunch turned into the lot with frequency, he'd parked in a fairly secluded spot. With Jillian's tinted windows, he probably couldn't be seen.

But neither could he see Sydney. She'd turned the radio back up and only when he opened the car door and stuck one foot out did she speak through the radio.

"Sit back, sweetheart. Relax. There's no need to go anywhere."

He swiveled around, but if Sydney was anywhere nearby—and he figured she was if she could see him—

she'd hidden that candy-apple-red car of hers extremely well.

"What are you up to, Sydney Colburn?" he asked rhetorically, waiting while she flipped through the radio stations, gave up and from the sound of it, slipped in a CD. He sat back in the driver's seat, but left the door open.

"Ooh, there we go," she said. "That's perfect. Smooth jazz. Saxophone. Remember that payback I owe you, Adam? Well, baby, here it is."

Music? No way. He knew she had something naughty in mind, because, well, with Sydney that was pretty much a given. He heard the rustle of material, and knew the sound had to be close to her breasts.

"Do you know what I'm doing, Adam? I'm unbuttoning my blouse. I'm wearing a black bra, lace cups. Soft lace, but it still chafes my nipples, especially when I'm sitting here, all alone, thinking about you—what you do to me, what you're going to do to me after I tell you where I'm hiding."

Adam slammed the car door shut and grabbed the steering wheel for support. Holy moly. Sydney was about to have phone sex with him. One-way phone sex, courtesy of Jillian's wiretap.

11

SYDNEY TOOK A DEEP BREATH, closed her eyes, and allowed the dulcet tones of the alto sax to wash over her. She knew the name of the business Kyle had called, and the revelation, she knew, would send Adam's investigation into emotional and physical hyperdrive. Without a doubt, plane tickets and heated confrontations were in her immediate future. But she knew they shouldn't make a move until they consulted Jillian, and she wasn't due back at the office for an hour. In the meantime, Sydney intended to use the time to deepen the connection between her and Adam by sharing a sexual fantasy she'd never fulfilled with any other man.

She pictured his face, with its incredible light brown eyes, straight nose, full lips and rugged chin. She imagined him as she'd first seen him the day before—shirtless, hot from a hard day's work, yet as comfortable in low-slung jeans as he'd once been in sleek Italian suits.

Habit caused her to focus first on his physical attributes, but she sighed, accepting that her attraction to him no longer centered on the bulk in the man's body or the truly unique color of his eyes. This Adam, the fighter, the survivor, the one who'd drummed his chest to protect her and worried about her safety, then used his logic and trust in her intelligence to support her through the somewhat risky interaction with Kyle. This man, the new one—or maybe just the one she finally, truly knew—spurred her to push beyond her few sensual limits to test unexplored territory.

Sure, she'd had phone sex once—with Adam, actually, when she'd been away at a writers' conference and needed a brand of sexual satisfaction more intense than anything she could accomplish alone. The sex had been thrilling, exciting, new. She'd wanted to relive that experience with Adam, but he didn't remember. Would never remember. She accepted that now. But it didn't mean she couldn't recreate the intimacy—with a fresh twist.

Through the windshield, she watched Adam slam the door shut on Jillian's Mustang. She'd found the parking space for the Corvette by luck, behind a low stone wall in a park across the street from the Hennessy Group, curtained by a weeping willow that was probably going to do a number on her paint job. Oh, well. It was just a car. What she and Adam would soon share would be worth so much more.

"I wore these clothes to be sexy for you, did you know that? Yeah, I'll bet Kyle got a thrill, but I didn't give a damn about him. It's you I want to make love with, Adam. Just you."

She wondered if he'd believe her, truly believe her, considering her past. But she'd made a promise to herself to never harbor regrets, and she wasn't going to start now. Her past made her who she was—a woman unafraid to push her sexuality to the edge, a woman unafraid to explore pleasure in any form that appealed to her. But she was also, until now, a woman who was not *afraid* to love, but was unprepared and unwilling to love. She cared about her sex partners, had even been friends with a few. But with Adam, all bets were off. She was playing in uncharted territory. And the rush propelled her to see how far this erotic exploration with Adam would take them.

"Are you wondering what I'm doing? I have my eyes closed, because I want to pretend my hands are your hands, that you're watching me. Close your eyes, Adam. Picture me in your mind."

Sydney paused. For the first time in recent memory, she questioned her ability to find the right words to evoke the emotions she needed Adam to feel. Her books were one thing. This was life. Love. Her heart. His. Deeper than desire, she wanted him to burn. Pushed beyond passion, she wanted him consumed by the single-minded need to be inside her, one with her, joined with her in body—and, soon, in soul.

ADAM FORCED his lids down over his eyes. He pressed a lever, easing his seat back, then turned up the volume on the radio, loud enough to block out street noise, but not so loud that someone who happened by would hear Sydney's sweet moans. He took a deep breath, exhaling slowly, forcing any apprehension out of his body. No one could see him. And since he couldn't see her, he chose to believe that no one else could, either. Despite the cars coming in and out of the parking lot behind him, despite the daylight shining through the tinted windows, he and Sydney were alone. Just the two of them. Sharing an intimacy that pushed him into startlingly new sexual territory.

As he waited, with only the sound of Sydney's sweet breathing adding lyrics to the sexy, instrumental jazz, he allowed himself to forget that she might know the identity of the people who stole his plans and tried to have him killed. He trusted that she withheld the name because once she revealed it, they would likely have to go separate ways, at least for a short time, while he continued the investigation on his own. He wouldn't allow her to step into real danger on his behalf. And until this chapter of his life was closed, he couldn't fully explore the possibilities of what he and Sydney could have in the future. How could they when he had no idea what that future might entail?

"Do you have a clear picture in your mind, Adam? My gold blouse is completely unbuttoned. My bra is black and lacy. Mmmm. I'm tracing the cup with my finger, teasing my skin, imagining you're touching me, arousing me."

Instinctively, he rolled his fingers into his slick palms. He remembered precisely how Sydney's breasts molded to his palm, round, soft, yet centered with hard peaks that seemed wired to the heart of her sexual desire. He imagined the feel, the taste, the sweet lavender scent she dusted over her skin, a translucent, perfumed powder dotted with tiny flecks of sparkle, shiny points only visible to a lover.

He heard a tiny click, the rustle of material.

"Oh, yeah. That's better. I feel so heavy, so hot. The wiretap itches, but I'm going to leave it in place. I don't want you to miss one bit of this. I'm going to touch my nipples now, baby. Just like you do. Squeezing between your thumb and forefinger, right before you pinch hard. Oh, yeah. Just like that."

Adam opened his mouth to pull in a deep, ragged breath. His erection strangled against his jeans and trickles of sweat danced down his spine. He opened his eyes long enough to check the air conditioner in the car, which, surprisingly, was still in working order. He listened, enthralled, as Sydney teased and plucked her sensitive flesh and related every nuance, every tendril of sexual excitement in a provocative play-by-play. Then she licked her fingers, wet her nipples and described with sensual detail how his mouth, as she imagined it, felt against her skin.

By the time she'd slipped her hands into her panties, Adam thought he'd lose his mind. He lowered the volume on Jillian's radio, glad no one but he could hear her moans of pleasure. He glanced outside the car. No one was around. When he thought he'd go mad with wanting, he noticed the binoculars he'd tossed on the passenger seat. He grabbed them and, with desperate precision, scanned the area around the offices until he caught a telltale flash of shiny red.

"I'm so close, Adam, so close."

He grinned. She was close all right—close enough for him to dash across the street and see to it that she didn't complete the job he should be doing. He turned off the car, locked and pocketed the keys, then snuck across the street to approach her vehicle from behind.

She nearly jumped out of her bare skin when he pulled open her unlocked door. A sweet flush pinkened her flesh, from the tips of her naked breasts to the inside of her parted thighs.

"Adam!"

He knelt down and pulled the car door as close to his body as he could. Slowly, he snaked a hand up her leg, his fingers searching for the hot moistness she'd so carefully described over the wiretap.

"You're a very bad girl, Sydney."

Her eyes lit up at the compliment. "Bad enough to make you want me?"

He slipped his fingers beyond the tiny triangle of her panties, already off center, already wet. "I want you, Sydney."

"For how long?"

Forever. But how could he make such a commitment, now, in the heat of lust, in the face of dizzying passion? None of the sexual chemistry between them changed the fact that he still had little to offer her beyond the sex, beyond the pleasure. But with a woman like her at his side 24/7, would he care?

He slid one finger inside her, watched her mold her body flush against the curved leather seat while the sensations shot over her. "For as long as it takes," he answered, pressing a second finger inside, stretching her, feeling the warm wetness of her flesh wrap possessively around his hand. "Will it take long?"

She grabbed the steering wheel, her arms tight as her body clenched around his skillful touch. He found her center and wasted no time in bringing her to the brink.

Her moans pleased him, her surrender to his power washed all his own need from his mind. He wanted only to hear her come. Wild and furious.

He wrapped his lips around her breast, then finished the job she'd started. Her cries echoed in his ears, her heat bathed him with pure, sexual release. When her breathing finally steadied and her gaze regained its focus, he wordlessly helped her dress.

She remained oddly silent. Only once she'd regained a semblance of normalcy did she meet his gaze and ask, "So, was that apt payback?"

"You don't owe me anything, Sydney. I owe you."

She shook her head, her gaze cast down. She didn't answer for a long minute and her silence prickled the hair along the back of his neck.

"Sydney?"

When she faced him again, her wicked smile had returned. But before he could gauge if the humor lit all the way to her eyes, she glanced aside to fiddle with her purse.

"Give a girl a minute to get herself together, okay?"

Perplexed, Adam stood and stared while she fixed her makeup, then decided to take a brief walk around the car. He'd either said something or done something to upset her, but he couldn't imagine what. He shook his head, figuring when she wanted him to know, she'd tell him. Sydney wasn't the type to play mind games, and what they'd shared had been intensely intimate. Maybe she'd finally bit off more than she could chew in the sex department, a thought that surged his pride more than he'd ever verbally admit.

She turned over the engine and rolled down her window.

"I'm going to move the car across the street. Wanna lift?"

Her sly smile had returned, along with that sassy glow that seemed to light her entire face. God, she was beautiful. And generous. And brave. And, at least for the moment, she was all his.

"I can walk. I want to make sure I locked Jillian's car correctly."

She put the car in Reverse and carefully backed out from the hiding place beneath the tree. "Suit yourself."

She eased the Corvette slowly over the dirt road, then waited for traffic to ease before she shot across the street. For a split second, he wondered if she'd considered leaving him. He didn't know why, but the suspicion sneaked out from somewhere deep in his gut, forcing him to frown for the first time since he'd run off with Sydney. Then he realized that even a bad girl like her wouldn't abandon him at this moment—when she knew the name of the person who'd tried to kill him.

He jogged across the street, rechecked the security of the Mustang, then strode to where she waited, leaning with her saucy backside against the driver's-side door of her car.

He suspected he should say something about their sexual adventure, but what? She'd already retreated from conversation once. Best to stick to the matter at hand for now.

"Did you get the name? Do you know who set me up?"

She nodded. "You're not going to like this information."

His chest tightened. "Can't be worse than not knowing at all. Besides, your little trick with the wiretap has made me one happy man. It's going to take something big to tear that down."

Her smile faded. "Then you'd better hold on tight, Adam. Kyle's call was to Malcolm and Associates in Baltimore."

SYDNEY WATCHED the disbelief, confusion and betrayal play over Adam's face like a grotesque mask, molded from clay in varying shades of beige, then pink, then red.

"Malcolm? Are you sure?"

She nodded. "The caller ID doesn't lie. Of course, we don't know who specifically at Malcolm that he spoke to. It might not have been Marcus himself."

Adam took a few steps backward, his hands dangling at his sides, his head shaking on repeatedly, as if "no" was the only thought he could process. Marcus Malcolm had been Adam's mentor in the architectural business. Marcus had shown Adam the ropes of the business, taught him to play golf, encouraged him to reach for the stars in his design goals.

Adam had spoken about the man just yesterday, with the type of glowing terms few men used to described another, particularly one who became a competitor. But, according to Adam, Marcus had called shortly after he'd returned home from rehab, had offered to help him get back on his feet. Adam had turned him down, but now Sydney wondered if old loyalty caused the older man to make such a generous offer...or had it been guilt?

"I can't believe Malcolm would be involved," he said finally, his eyes hard, his voice harder.

"I'm not saying he was." Purely out of instinct, she raised her hands in front of her. "Don't shoot the messenger, Adam. All we know is that Kyle called someone at that firm."

He turned toward the Mustang, then stopped. Marching back, he tossed her the keys and headed toward the office.

"Where are you going?"

"Back to Homosassa first. Then to Baltimore."

"Without me?"

She'd made an assumption based entirely on his hasty departure, but her words stopped him dead. When he turned, the look on his face verified her suspicion. He meant to confront his old boss and he meant to do it alone.

"No more cloak-and-dagger for you, Sydney. Someone from that firm tried to have me killed. I won't involve you."

"I'm already involved."

"We both heard what Kyle said. As long as you lay low, no one is going after you. You might want to warn your attorney, though."

Sydney laughed. "My attorney used to be a county judge. Before that, he played fullback for the Buccaneers. His firm is the largest in the city. Besides, if anyone tries to find the plans at his office, they won't. They don't exist. But you, you exist. And I won't let you walk into this alone."

"You don't have any say in the matter." Adam turned on his heel and shot through the door to the Hennessy Group office without a backward glance.

Sydney froze, not so much wounded as shocked.

He was kidding, right? He didn't seriously think she was going to let him call a cab to haul his sorry, sexy ass all the way back to the farm and then book a flight to Baltimore to confront his mentor alone, did he? Without her? Was her bad-girl persona completely lost on the man?

Duh.

Sydney stalked inside just as he punched numbers into the receptionist's phone. Without hesitating, she flattened the button on the receiver and disconnected the call.

"Sydney."

Her name was said in warning, but she refused to back down, despite the tick that had developed in his ruggedly square jaw.

"Adam."

She matched his tone, then upped the tension with a smile.

"This isn't a joke. This is my future."

"Technically, no. It's your past. I'm your future."

With tight lips, he put the phone down, grabbed her elbow and pulled her to a quiet corner of the empty reception area.

"Don't do this, Sydney. Not now."

"Do what?"

Her feigned innocence made a vein throb at his left temple.

"Make decisions about *us* until I've sorted out this mess."

She laid her hand softly on his shoulder. "That's fine. I totally understand that you need to put this to rest. But there's no reason you have to do it without me."

She placed a finger over his mouth before he could go on again about the danger.

"Just because I go with you to Baltimore doesn't mean I have to go with you when you confront Malcolm," she clarified. "I want to be nearby, though. I need to be. Like I should have been a year ago."

Slowly, her honest confession worked past his anger. She watched the tension in his shoulders drip down out of his hands, which he wrapped around her. Pulling her close, he buried his nose in her hair, nuzzling. The gesture nearly toppled her—so sweet, so simple, so brimming with loving emotion, she thought she might cry.

"You're a brave woman, Sydney Colburn."

She shook her head. Her knees wobbled, and for the first time since she'd concocted her scheme to lure Adam back into her life, she wondered if she had the intestinal fortitude to carry her through the rough spots, the scary spots. Like now, facing down what could be real love without running or flinching or showing any sign of the fear ravaging through her veins.

"Not so brave," she answered. "More like stubborn."

"I can't argue that."

She knocked him in the shoulder with a fist, knowing she couldn't argue, either, and not knowing what else to say. The emotions of the afternoon ran such a wide gamut, she figured she'd best slip into a safe operating mode until she worked out exactly what she was feeling, what she was thinking. Did they really have a future? Did she really love him?

"What say you check in with the receptionist and see if Jillian is back," she suggested. "She could give us some advice on how to best handle this turn of events. I'll use my cell phone and make plane reservations. When do you want to leave?"

"As soon as we can."

Adam glanced over at the door, and Sydney could see the longing. He wanted to fly to Baltimore now, face down his past. So he could finally plan a real future?

Sydney headed out the door, back to the cell phone which she'd left in the car. *As soon as we can.* Sounded like a plan to her. The sooner Adam unraveled the mystery of his past, the sooner she'd have his undivided attention regarding matters of the heart.

12

THE SIGN READ, FLANAGAN'S PUB. Sydney headed straight for the door, knowing of no friendlier place in the world than a neighborhood bar named for someone Irish. Before leaving to meet with the Baltimore detective who'd agreed to provide Adam with some unofficial help, Adam had instructed her to hang tight. He'd wanted to do this on his own. He'd *insisted*. But she figured he also wanted to make sure he didn't expose her to any potential danger. She guessed she could have objected, could have insisted she was a big girl who could take care of herself—but he knew that. In only two days, he'd managed to show her how much he respected her intelligence and quick thinking, which made her love him all the more. Damn. Sydney Colburn in love. Imagine that.

She knew she loved the man when she realized she understood Adam's need to orchestrate this confrontation on his own, no matter how it contradicted her need to feel as if they were a team. And darn it if, during their consultation, Jillian hadn't agreed with Adam that Sydney shouldn't put herself at risk. Sydney's only peace of mind came from the fact that Jillian had also strongly suggested that Adam finally contact the Tampa Police detective who'd originally investigated his case.

Thankfully, the man had not only remembered Adam, but he'd also agreed to interview Kyle immediately since their eavesdropped conversation led Adam to suspect the plans would soon be sold to a foreign company. The task of proving a theft with international players would be daunting. With that in mind, the detective also called an old contact on the Baltimore police force, one who owed him a favor. Adam was going in alone, but he had professionals charting and monitoring his every move.

That was the only reason she nixed the compulsion to do what one of her heroines might—secretly follow him. Luckily, Sydney accepted that those heroines usually ended up paying a big price for their arrogant haphazardness. The consequences always caused the character to grow in some meaningful way, but Sydney didn't want to grow; she wanted a drink. She'd done a damn good bit of growing while making the simple decision to pursue Adam again. Now that she knew she wanted him for the long haul, she'd have to play the game his way. For now.

Fortunately, Adam hadn't designated where he preferred she do her hanging, so Flanagan's Pub it was. He had a cell phone and so did she. And Flanagan's was only one block from Malcolm and Associates' architectural offices. If he needed her, wanted her, whatever...she'd be close by, in a pub comfortably warm and inviting after the lunchtime rush.

As she had suspected, Flanagan's was an old-time bar, from the pocked wood floors to the sticky booths and absence of anything remotely identifiable as trendy. No neon in this place. Any and all advertisements for beer and whiskey, the two staples, were carved and painted on wood or drawn on chalkboard. The polished bar top and brass fixtures gleamed beside clean glasses and frosty mugs. And since the curved-back barstools looked more inviting than some dark booth in the corner, Sydney ponied up at the bar. She smiled when the bartender, a voluptuous, six-foot-tall Amazon whose thick red hair made Sydney's darker auburn shade look downright mousy, turned around and grinned right back. In a Jessica Rabbit T-shirt and tight jeans, the woman holding the dishrag immediately struck Sydney as a true kindred spirit. Bad and lovin' it.

"Cool shirt," Sydney complimented. She twisted in her seat, not entirely comfortable in the attire she'd chosen, an emerald-green, wraparound Versace with sheer hose and slim Vera Wang heels. If she couldn't be useful, the least she could be was sexy. Adam hadn't had an easy time abandoning her in their suite after he'd watched her dress. Particularly since she'd worn his favorite black thong panties. Served him right.

"You don't look like the T-shirt type," the bartender said, her gaze intensely doubtful.

Sydney laughed. "Believe me, sister, I don't dress this way every day. And I certainly don't do it for myself."

The bartender arched a brow.

Sydney recanted. "Okay, so I do, a little. But I appreciate a soft pair of jeans and a snappy T-shirt as much as any girl, particularly one with Miss Jessica on it. I'd like to think I have a lot in common with her. Not bad, just drawn that way."

The bartender grinned, poured Sydney a neat whiskey that she hadn't ordered yet desperately appreciated, and slid it in front of her. "Ditto. My name's Venus," the server introduced. "Venus Messina."

Sydney shook the woman's proffered hand. "Sydney. Sydney Colburn."

"Sydney Colburn...no kidding? The writer?"

Grinning, Sydney took a tentative sip of the alcohol, and finding the blend smooth, shot back a generous gulp. "One and the same."

Venus leaned on the bar, her smile genuine, if not a little bit sad around the edges of her wine-colored lips. "That's awesome. I've read your stuff. Very hot. Especially those big hottie knights of yours. Too bad more men can't live up to your standard. And my favorite thing about your book—no wimpy heroines!"

Sydney sighed. Adam not only lived up to her heroic standards, he surpassed them. Since she set her books in historical periods, the men of her literary fantasies swung broadswords and rode stallions, wore chain mail and generally cursed the day her strong, capable, beautiful heroines burst into their lives. On the surface, her personal knight in shining armor had little in common with the alpha males who populated her stories. But Sydney knew the truth. Adam embodied every aspect of her perfect man. He always had.

Where her battle-hungry heroes wielded swords, Adam had his rapier wit, his keen intelligence. Where her fictional men thirsted for battle, Adam had salivated over success in his chosen field.

That thought stopped her comparison, tingeing her musings with sadness. If he didn't get his plans back, if he didn't figure out what had happened that awful night last year that had robbed him of his most cherished skill, where would that leave him?

She wanted him in her life no matter what, but she knew he wanted more. He'd told her so. He wanted his career back, his masterpiece. And he'd made no secret that until he'd accomplished this task, he would make no plans for the future. Leaving her...where? In love and waiting for the perfect man—and Sydney's worst skill was patience.

"Men who meet my standard do exist," Sydney finally responded, sipping her whiskey with care. "The trouble is finding them."

"Finding men has never been a problem for me," Venus noted. "Keeping them? That's another story."

"The good ones or the so-so ones?" Sydney asked. She'd had her share of so-so, by choice rather than any difficulty finding the higher quality version. She gravitated toward men who didn't challenge her, didn't do anything that might inspire her to reflect on the shallowness of her life. She hadn't come to that conclusion until recently, but that didn't make it any less true. A man of quality like Adam had slipped into her life entirely by accident.

Or perhaps Fate had lent a hand?

"Good or even so-so wouldn't be bad. Unfortunately, the only ones I seem to manage to hang on to are the creeps who cost you jobs or empty your bank accounts. Not the green-eyed dreamboats with chestnut hair and the kind of wicked, sexy grin that ought to be illegal."

Venus leaned on the bar, her gaze caught in the great

far-off region known as fantasyland. Or perhaps she toyed with a memory? After just a few seconds, darkness fell over the bartender's wistful gaze, like an intermission curtain during the best part of a play.

"Uh-oh," Sydney said, finishing her whiskey.

"What?"

"You got it bad, sister."

"Speak for yourself."

Laughing, Sydney pushed her glass toward the bartender and nodded for a second round. "I *am* speaking for myself. I've got it badder than most. Hell, I *am* badder than most, and still I'm sitting here drinking with you, wondering if the next time my cell phone rings, the man in my life will be preparing me for that ultimate goodbye."

Venus nodded while she flipped a dark bottle over Sydney's glass, manipulating the stream of amber with a seasoned hand. "We bad girls have it tough, you know? Those goody two-shoes have saying 'no' down to an art form, blaming morals or past hurts! We say yes, because of those *same* morals and past hurts! We can't seem to give up on the idea that the next handsome stud who comes along might erase what the last one did."

"Handsome studs are a dime a dozen."

That came from a low, sultry voice down the bar. Sydney turned in time to notice a striking brunette, dressed all in black despite the summer temperatures, nursing a beer. Wow. Sydney considered herself incredibly observant. Either she'd been utterly distracted by her situation with Adam and her conversation with

Venus, or this chick knew how to blend into the woodwork.

Venus stood straight and started rubbing her dish towel over the bar, making her way closer to the Angelina Jolie look-alike in the corner. "Hell, girl. I almost forgot you were here. Come join us. Bad girls need to stick together."

Wariness played over the woman's face, but after a moment's hesitation she picked up her drink and moved over next to Sydney.

Venus snorted. "Last club I belonged to was the Girl Scouts. I got kicked out when I was eleven." As Sydney raised a questioning brow, Venus explained. "Summer camp. I got caught sneaking into the boys' cabin to play Seven Minutes In Heaven. The troop leader came in just as I was heading into the closet with Tommy Callahan." She shook her head and sighed at the memory. "He had the cutest dimples. And cool braces."

Sydney nodded. She remembered a similar metal-mouthed lothario in her childhood.

"I never made it past Brownies," the woman in black admitted. "I kept altering the uniform in a way that, well, didn't exactly meet with the troop leader's approval. But the boys liked it." She winked. "Besides, brown isn't my color."

"Hell," Sydney confessed, "my mother never let me forget I got tossed out of preschool for showing the boys my underwear."

Venus snickered. "Hey, why was she complaining?"

"Yeah," the brunette said with a knowing look at Venus. They finished the thought in unison. "At least you were wearing 'em."

After a round of introductions that identified the woman as Nicole Bennett, Sydney ordered two more whiskeys, one for her new pal Nicole, and one for Venus, who'd decided it was high time she took a break.

"I guess we've been members of the bad girls club since birth, huh?" Venus asked.

Sydney nodded. Maybe not from birth, but close to it. "So what's a bad girl to do?" she wondered aloud. She didn't regret her lifestyle choices, nor did she wish she could undo any of her past. But what her bad-girl attitude had done was leave her totally unprepared for a real relationship. When she'd first set out to lure Adam back into her life, she'd thought caring about him and showing him how much she desired him would be enough to prove how her attitude had changed, how much she wanted to change. But he didn't remember her, much less her former attitude. And in the past two days, she'd utilized all her powers, feminine or otherwise, to give him a true glimpse of the real Sydney. A resourceful, smart, sexy and caring woman who'd pull out all the stops in pursuit of her man. And yet she had absolutely no confidence that, either with his recovered plans or without them, Adam would want her in his life for the long haul.

Venus snapped to attention and made a humorous wisecrack when two straight-laced women entered and joined the suits at the table. After taking their order, she returned to their conversation. "So what's a bad girl to do?" Venus repeated Sydney's question, clear from her tone that she possessed no answer.

"Mend her ways?" Nicole volunteered, smirking.

"No way. Took me too long to realize that I like who I am," Venus insisted.

Sydney nodded. "I agree. Good girls are highly overrated. Not that I know this from experience," she clarified.

Nicole mulled that over, then threw back the whiskey like an old pro. "Maybe the reformation should depend on what kind of bad girl a woman has been?"

Venus's beautifully sculpted eyebrows pulled together. "There's more than one kind?"

Sydney glanced at Nicole. Oh, yeah. Bad girls came in as many varieties as nail polish and condoms. This one had a dark gleam in her gray eyes, as if her status as a bad girl stemmed from something more serious than taking lots of lovers or forgetting to apologize for outrageous behavior because you didn't give a damn about what other people thought.

"Absolutely," Sydney answered. "I think the key is to keep the part of the badness you enjoy—in my case, my addiction to incredible sex—and toss out the rest. Hey, we're women of the new millennium. We can change anything about ourselves, anytime we like."

As if to add a musical accompaniment to her grand decree, Sydney's cell phone filled the quiet bar with a trilling rendition of George Thorogood's "Bad to the Bone." The women laughed, containing their chuckles while Sydney answered.

"Adam?"

"No, this is Detective Bransom of the Baltimore Police Department."

Sydney's heart stopped dead in her chest. Her face

must have paled, because Venus grabbed her hand and Nicole leaned in close.

She somehow recovered her ability to speak. "Is Adam all right?"

"Yes, ma'am, as far as we know. But he wanted me to call you as soon as everything was in place. He said you'd probably be nearby."

Sydney released a pent-up sigh as Venus and Nicole continued their conversation. "I'm around the corner at Flanagan's."

The detective chuckled. "Tell Joe to ice up a brew for me. I'm off duty today and will be stopping by as soon as your boyfriend gets what he needs."

"You think he will?"

"Never know. He's one determined guy. Don't see how anyone could keep him from getting what he wants."

"Yeah, I know the type."

Intimately. As in, she was the same way. She promised to meet the detective, parked in his dark blue sedan across from the architectural firm's offices, in ten minutes. She disconnected the call, then pulled her wallet out of her purse and tossed a hundred-dollar bill beside her drink, which she drained.

Venus stared at the face of Benjamin Franklin, before swiping the bill off the bar. "I'll get your change."

"Keep it. Use some to get Nicole as good and drunk as she wants to be. Use the rest to buy yourself something fun. I wish I could stick around, but duty calls."

She slipped off the barstool and straightened her dress.

"Duty? That doesn't sound like a concern for a bad girl," Nicole joked, her tone wry.

Sydney gave that a long thought, wishing she had more time to chat and deconstruct Nicole's psyche. The woman could make a great character for a book. Instead, she smiled. "Depends on what that duty entails, doesn't it?"

Behind her, the door from the street opened, flashing bright light into the darkened bar. Sydney turned and, for an instant, experienced that familiar tingle she'd trained herself to feel whenever a handsome hunk was within flirting distance.

But despite the man's tanned skin, chestnut hair, lose-yourself-in-them green eyes and incredibly kissable lips, the thrill quickly faded. Sydney couldn't have been happier. No other guy was going to do it for her anymore, no matter how tall, dark or handsome. She waved one last time at Venus, who stared, mesmerized by the stud who'd entered. Then Sydney turned her attention to Nicole, who watched the bartender with sardonic amusement. With a feminine shimmy to set her rhythm in motion, Sydney walked out into the daylight.

She didn't know what Adam wanted from their relationship, and she believed one hundred percent that he didn't know, either. Too much of his future was invested, purposefully or accidentally, in the situation with his missing plans. She hadn't pressed him too hard, but something in her gut told her the time had come for a serious conversation. By this evening, he'd know more about the plans and have a clearer direction for his life.

And if he didn't, Sydney decided she'd just have to draw the guy a map. She wanted him. Now, and for the long run. She loved him. Foreign as the concept might have sounded to her two days ago, she faced that realization with the same bottom-line attitude that had brought her this far in life. Far enough to finally see what she really wanted was Adam. And, damn it, what Sydney Colburn wanted, Sydney Colburn got.

ADAM BLEW OUT a deep breath, clutched the brass handles on the office doors and propelled himself toward his future. Just before entering, he'd dialed Detective Bransom on his cell phone, made sure the man had found Sydney, then tossed the active phone in his suit pocket without disconnecting. His cell wasn't one of Jillian's nifty listening devices, but the phone wasn't illegal, either. There was no law against accidentally leaving your cell phone on, just as there was no law against a friend of a friend happening to overhear something that went on in the background. Bransom assured him this loophole might not hold up in court, but, at this point, Adam didn't give a damn.

Malcolm and Associates took up the two lower floors of an office building they'd designed and built over twenty years ago. Despite two decades, the glass gleamed, the chrome shined and the leather furniture reflected the wealth, success and good taste that Marcus Malcolm prized. Adam thought of the man as his mentor. He'd taken Adam on as an unpaid intern during college, then offered him a dream job the minute he'd earned his degree.

Though Adam had had a supportive father back

home, Marcus had pinch-hit the role during the time Adam had spent in Maryland. Back in Florida, Frank Brody had taught his son about honesty, integrity and how to build a sturdy structure with your own two hands. In Maryland, Marcus Malcolm had taught him how to incorporate honesty and integrity into the business of designing sturdy structures with your mind and imagination. Adam, young and hungry to splash into the architectural world in a big way, had eaten up everything Malcolm had said to him.

That Malcolm could be involved in the theft made no sense to Adam. Attempted murder was too much to contemplate. But he didn't have much of a choice but to investigate, not if he intended to reclaim at least part of the life he'd lost thanks to the accident.

"May I help you?"

The pretty receptionist smiled, her hair a bouncy brunette, no recognition in her blue eyes. Adam figured he might run into people who knew him from the past, but this college-age woman wasn't one of them.

"I'm an old friend of Mr. Malcolm. I was wondering if I could sneak on past and surprise him."

Despite her young, naive smile, she instantly eyed him with suspicion. "I don't think so. But if you give me your name, I could call him and see if he's free."

At least he knew now that Marcus was in the building and not off supervising a job site or traveling, allowing his son, Steven, to run the show. While Adam and Steven had been approximately the same age, the two had never had much in common. Adam wouldn't go so far as to have considered Steven a rival—from day one, Adam had understood that Steven would inherit his father's business and Adam would go on to start his own, closer to home in Florida. He glanced over at the oil portrait hanging behind the reception desk featuring Steven sitting in a stately leather chair, his father to his side, Malcolm's hand possessively on his shoulder. Adam now wondered, though, if what he had considered a strictly professional relationship between two young architects with divergent goals could have been a rivalry.

A rivalry that had led to theft? Attempted murder? Why? Why would the heir to a veritable empire steal from him? What could Steven have had to gain except money, which he already had boatloads of? Steven's involvement made no more sense than Malcolm's, and yet the call Kyle had placed had routed through this office. Through the same phone system the young receptionist was about to use now.

Adam thought fast. He didn't want Marcus to know he was there ahead of time, certain the element of surprise was still his best bet to gauge an honest response. But he also hadn't wanted to confront Marcus somewhere outside the building, like at his car or his home. If the plans were in his possession, they'd be here. In the office.

"How about you call Linda? She's still around, right? Tell her an old friend is here, but that I want to surprise Marcus. She'll play along."

He leaned one hand on the receptionist's desk, his body and tone amplifying the casual confidence he wanted to portray. For added emphasis, he turned on one of those charming smiles that always worked so well with Renée.

The girl batted her eyelashes.

Bingo.

"Have a seat. I'll see if Linda's at her desk."

Adam saved his triumphant smile for after he'd turned his back and headed over toward the couch. He'd taken several risks. First, he had no idea if Linda was still Marcus's secretary, but had decided to take a guess. Linda was Marcus's wife's sister, and according to him, the best secretary in the business. Even ten years ago, she'd operated as his right hand. He couldn't imagine the two ever professionally parting ways under normal circumstances.

Now that he knew she was still around, he had a second risk to face. He trusted that if Marcus had indeed involved himself in, or even orchestrated, the attack against Adam, he wouldn't have involved Linda. Marcus wasn't an idiot and while Adam had trouble imagining him party to a crime, he had more difficulty swallowing that Marcus would have made Linda an accessory.

The door to the inner office opened, and Linda came out, her eyes widening with glee the moment she saw him. She held her arms outstretched and squealed.

"Oh, my Lord! I can't believe you're here!"

Adam grinned, then joined her and let her wrap her arms around him in a hug.

"It's great to see you, Linda."

She pulled back, but kept her grip on his shoulders. "Great to see me? Who cares? I didn't nearly die on some dark road." She turned him around, then hugged him one more time.

Adam felt a lump form in his throat. No way was she

faking this response. She was honestly happy and surprised to see him.

"Where have you been? Marcus talks about you all the time, you know. We're finally building that town center down in Asheville—the one you worked on. Gosh, who can believe it's been ten years?"

Adam did remember the retro-Colonial structure since the building had been one of his first solo projects after joining the firm. He knew that years often passed between the design of a building and the actual construction, particularly when a city government was involved, but ten years seemed a lifetime away, even with five years missing in between.

"Not me. You don't look a day older."

She slapped him on the shoulder. "Flirt! You always were the charmer. I can't wait until Marcus sees you. He's going to be so surprised."

I'll bet.

She tucked her arm in his and led him back into the offices, chattering away uncharacteristically. He remembered Linda as serious, always concentrating on one project or another. Then again, she hadn't been dour or anything. She'd been quick to laugh and foil his attempts at teasing. As she wound them over to a private elevator and pressed the up button, Adam accepted that her surprise and excitement over seeing him again was genuine.

But the minute they stepped onto the plush carpet outside the suite of offices on the second floor, he knew not everyone at Malcolm and Associates harbored the same nostalgic happiness. As he strode up and met Steven Malcolm eye-to-eye, his former colleague paled, then sneered.

"Brody? What the hell are you doing here?"

13

"I DON'T LIKE THE SOUND OF THAT." Sydney lurched forward in the passenger seat of Carl Bransom's unmarked police car, her hand clutching the dash. He'd perched his cell phone just above the radio, the speaker phone option turned on. The voices were muffled and crackly, but Sydney knew sharp enmity when she heard it.

"Relax, Ms. Colburn," Detective Bransom said, his beefy palm pushing softly on her shoulder. "Unless someone threatens him with bodily harm, we're sitting tight."

Sydney snapped a glance at the man's hand, which he quickly and smartly removed. She watched him settle back comfortably against the worn fake-leather seat, munching on an apple, acting as if the world could fly straight to hell and he wouldn't move one overbulked muscle.

"You can sit tight all you want, Detective. It's not my style." She reached for the door handle. Despite the man's laid-back attitude and Arnold Schwarzenegger physique, he had her arm in a tight grip almost instantaneously.

"Now, Ms. Colburn, that wouldn't be a good idea."

Sydney hissed between clenched teeth, but knew the man was right. He allowed her to yank free, then folded her arms over her chest. She had to let Adam do this. As long as she remained in the car, she could at least hear the conversation. If she barged into the offices and disrupted things, Adam's plan would sink faster than a stone in a puddle.

"Steven," she heard Adam answer, his voice garbled by the movement of his cell phone inside his pocket. "Long time no see."

Sydney closed her eyes, trying to imagine the warm, inviting smile on Adam's face, the charming glint in those balmy brown eyes, the amazing fit of his broad shoulders in the sleek Italian suit they'd rescued from the cabin and had retailored to his new and improved bod right before their flight. She listened as Adam employed his smooth voice to defuse the hostility in Steven Malcolm. He'd barely mentioned the man when they'd talked about Marcus. But darn if Steven hadn't sounded shocked and, more significantly, angry to see him.

Luckily, in a matter of minutes, they were on their way in to see the big guy himself. Marcus Malcolm. The man who ran the show. The man who'd had a strong influence on Adam during the formative years of his career.

The man who may or may not have ordered someone to mow Adam down and leave him for dead on a dark, quiet road. Sydney shook her head, and forced her anger and indignation aside. She trusted Adam to take care of this situation on his own terms. How could she not when she also trusted him with the most valuable thing in her possession, her heart?

"Got something else sweet I can munch on in this

car?" she asked, her voice resigned. "Preferably something chocolate. A doughnut, maybe?"

So much for stereotypes. Bransom chuckled, popped open a cooler he kept behind his seat, and handed her a shiny green Granny Smith. Sydney took an incensed bite, then worked out her frustration by chewing like the fruit was her last meal.

ALMOST UNCONSCIOUSLY, Adam patted his pocket, hoping the cell phone hadn't lost the signal. The minute he'd stepped off the elevator, he'd spotted Steven. The animosity the man had for him couldn't have been stronger. The element of surprise had indeed given him insight. Steven Malcolm hated him, and he had no idea why.

But he couldn't very well excuse himself right now and try to call Meg to find out if he and Steven had had any kind of fight during his five forgotten years. He had to think on his feet. Damn. He really did wish he'd brought Sydney along though. If nothing else, she'd probably recognize the missing plans faster than he could, since he'd done the bulk of the work during his five forgotten years and nothing of the design remained in his brain except the first blue-ink pen sketch.

But the moment he haphazardly glanced into the conference room adjacent to Marcus's office, his heart stopped at what he saw.

"Adam, Marcus is right through here," Linda said, her arm outstretched toward a decorative archway that led toward Malcolm's two inner offices.

Adam glanced at Steven, who'd gone white as plaster again, obviously aware of what Adam had seen.

Their eyes clashed, but Adam fought to keep his penetrating glare from casting accusations. He just looked—hard—willing Steven to screw up and say something revealing.

Steven's jaw tensed, but he said nothing.

Adam matched his silence, but forced his shoulders to relax. He slipped his hands into the pockets of his pants, jingling the change he'd tossed in after buying a coffee from a vendor on the street. He thought about Sydney, wondered what the witty, resourceful woman would do in this situation—and decided that seducing the truth from Steven was out of the question. But the mental picture made him smile, causing Steven's forehead to erupt in moisture.

"Adam?" Linda called again.

"I'd rather meet Marcus right here, Linda. Why don't you call him out?"

Linda's gaze darted from Steven to Adam, taking in the tension between the two men. Without another word, she disappeared beyond the archway, calling to Marcus in a voice he'd best describe as urgent.

Good. He had them off guard. He also had them redhanded...although he still didn't know for certain who among them had been involved.

Adam didn't look back into the room. He didn't need to. In one glance, he'd memorized the scene. The plans he'd drawn were posted all over the walls, different angles, different views. A computer in the corner flashed a three-dimensional model on a twenty-four-inch screen. Manila files and presentation folders were stacked across the table, as if the staff had either recently met to discuss his design or would soon.

He stared at Steven, but he didn't say a word. When Marcus emerged, looking just as fit as any sixty-year-old man who played tennis every day should, Adam allowed a genuine grin to spread over his face. He had to trust his gut. And his gut said that Marcus knew nothing about what his son had done.

"Adam!"

His hearty handshake was followed by a hug.

"I was wondering when you were going to show up here, claim your share of what is going to be our crowning deal this year."

"My share?"

Marcus kept his arm around Adam's shoulder and led him into the conference room, every inch the proud businessman showing off his wares.

"Of course! I have a cashier's check that's been waiting for you ever since we sold the design to Malaysia. I added a second one when they hired us to implement and supervise the construction. You'll be very comfortable, Adam."

"I doubt that."

"Excuse me?"

Marcus had been reaching for a coffee carafe, but when he turned and faced Adam, his expression completely perplexed, Adam knew his mentor had no idea what had really happened. No time like the present to tell him the truth, but he wanted Steven inside, not lingering in the hall as he still was, his feet seemingly rooted to the spot.

"Call Steven inside, Marcus. And you might want to send Linda on an errand. We're long overdue for a conversation."

He didn't know if his requests were wise, but he knew he had to expedite a confrontation. He wasn't about to take a percentage of a fortune that should be his and his alone. *He* should have been the one who sold the design. *He* should have been the one hired to supervise construction and to deal with the invariable glitches that no architect could anticipate until someone started pounding the steel and pouring the mortar. This was *his* project, *his* showpiece.

He took a quick glance around the room. Yes, he recognized the basic design, but, beyond that, the plans were little more than blue line drawings on grayish white sheets.

He cursed. The blueprints were useless to him. Beyond making a sale, he no longer had the skill or expertise to handle the duties of a lead architect. But that wasn't his concern right now. Couldn't be. He had to deal with Steven, with the lies he'd told, with the plot he'd hatched.

"Steven, come in here."

Marcus's bark brooked no hesitation. Steven scurried inside, his gaze sweeping every corner of the room without meeting the eyes of his father or of Adam. In a gentler voice, Marcus asked Linda to make lunch reservations at a nearby upscale bistro.

"What's this all about, Adam?" Marcus took his seat at the head of the table, then motioned for Adam to sit beside him.

Adam shook his head. "I think maybe Steven needs to be the one to explain."

This time, Steven couldn't look away. "I have no idea what you're talking about."

Adam chuckled. That ruse wouldn't last long. "Steven, don't insult either one of us. You're caught. The police in Tampa are at this very minute interviewing a young man named Kyle Sanderson. Remember him? I think you might have spoken with him yesterday on the phone. You might be interested to know that he's retained an incredibly expensive, amazingly efficient attorney who is likely to broker a very nice immunity deal for his client in exchange for his knowledge about how you got your greedy, bloody hands on my design."

"Bloody? Adam, what the hell are you talking about?" Marcus demanded.

Adam's voice remained surprisingly calm. "Ask Steven."

"Steven?"

Just then, Adam's pocket trilled. His cell phone. Damn. He must have lost the connection.

"Excuse me," he said, not moving a muscle while he answered the call. "Hello?"

"Hey, hot stuff. Might want to check your equipment next time before you get to the good part of the interrogation."

Sydney's voice rumbled through the phone like warm, sugary molasses.

"My equipment seems to be fine now, thanks to you."

"Well, damn, I hope we're not still talking about your cell phone."

"Not entirely."

Her chuckle surged his blood. Here he was, about to confront the man who had stolen his future, and Adam couldn't help but anticipate the next time he'd make love with Sydney.

"Well, you're doing good. Go ahead and pocket us. I can think of worse places to hide."

Adam pretended to disconnect the call, but, this time, he decided to hold the phone in his hand rather than risk the connection dying again by being bounced around inside his jacket.

"Sorry about that. Important call. You were saying, Steven?"

"I wasn't saying anything. And I'm not going to."

Adam arched his eyebrows. "You think? You might want to consider the fact that I am completely physically recovered, Steven, no thanks to you. I'm stronger, quicker. Angrier. Now, I may not be able to design buildings anymore, but it doesn't take someone with perfect visual perception to calculate that before you can get your scrawny, lying, murderous ass out the door, I'll have my hands wrapped around your throat."

Adam raised his left hand, slowly fisting and releasing his long fingers. "I work in construction now, did you know that?"

Marcus had remained silent during the threatening exchange, but he stood, took Steven by the shoulder and pushed him down into a chair.

"Maybe I should start," Marcus volunteered.

Adam's eyes widened, his heart skipped a beat. "You knew about this? You know Steven stole my plans and nearly had me killed?"

"What?"

Nope. He definitely didn't know.

"That wasn't supposed to happen," Steven insisted. "Not like that."

Adam fought the urge to punch the table in lieu of Steven's face. "Don't blame Kyle for the accident, Steven. I know he knew nothing about it."

"You're right, he didn't. But neither did I," Steven admitted. "You weren't supposed to get hurt. You were so damned stubborn! I offered you the deal of a lifetime and you just couldn't give me a break."

"You offered me a deal?"

"A damned good one. Malcolm and Associates has the best connections in the business. I knew I could sell your plans for ten times what you could find on your own. My commission would have been more than I'd ever make drawing. I'm a better businessman than architect, but you couldn't help me out, couldn't make the money flow a little easier."

"What money?" Marcus asked.

"The money I offered him for his design." His stare speared through his father's horrified expression. "You told me yourself how much you wished Brody was still your protégé, that you'd have loved for him to have designed that building while he was still working for us."

"So you stole it from him?"

"I took possession in hopes of convincing him that my offer was more than generous. He wasn't supposed to nearly get himself killed."

"That's what happens when you hire someone to hit me from behind."

Steven glanced aside, neither verifying nor denying his complicity in the hit-and-run. And Adam had no recollection of Steven's approaching him, and he must not have taken the offer seriously if neither Meg nor his attorney had reminded him of the episode. But something didn't make sense. Steven would have known about the plans, but he couldn't have known when Adam had finally completed the design.

"How did you know I'd finished?"

Steven rolled his eyes. "I made a contact with the developer who'd made your initial bid."

"How'd you get Kyle involved?"

Crossing his arms over his chest, Steven sighed as if bored. Fear and wariness left his face, replaced with pure unadulterated loathing. "I knew the plans would go out by courier. I had my associates staked out at both your office and your home. With the money I was offering, I could buy off anyone."

Adam couldn't believe Steven so readily answered, but the man always had been an arrogant son of a bitch. He probably figured Adam couldn't go to the police with only his word of Steven's confession. Steven probably trusted Marcus to lie for him. Adam wondered, then decided to go for broke.

"Names, Steven. Who are these associates?"

Marcus stood, his hands slamming on the conference table. "Shut your mouth, boy. Don't say another word."

Adam cursed. "He nearly had me killed, Marcus. For money, which he already has plenty of, thanks to you. I deserve a complete explanation."

Marcus hesitated, shifting from foot to foot. He wiped his forehead, tightening his salt-and-pepper brow and emphasizing the lines on his face. His shoulders slumped. "Steven isn't capable of murder."

"He's right," Steven insisted. "Once I had the plans from Kyle, I gave orders for them to trash your office, maybe make you disappear for a little while, until you could see how lucrative my deal would be for both of us. But you—"

"I said shut up!" Marcus bellowed.

With each increase in Marcus's volume, the old man's strength wavered. Adam knew this was the moment to go for the kill, but he couldn't override his respect for his mentor, his compassion for the conflict undoubtedly raging through him right now for the son who'd betrayed him and the former protégé who deserved a fair shake.

Marcus bashed the button on the phone. "Linda, call my attorney. Tell him to get down here."

Marcus shook, the color of his face changing from a healthy pink to a rage-induced ruby. Though a chair was just behind him, he remained standing.

"You can't stop the truth from coming out, Marcus," Adam pointed out. "He almost had me killed. He stole my life's greatest work. Hell, he robbed me of my future as an architect. He's going to pay, Marcus. I'll make sure of that."

Marcus's face twisted in disgust. "Steven's a fool. He always has been, always will be. If he'd had half an ounce of the natural talent you had, he'd never have become so jealous. But he's still my son. I'm responsible."

Adam's chest tightened. "Did you know about this?"

"Of course not! But I should have known, should

have understood that you'd never sell out to us. Took a damned long time for him to convince me that you'd hired him to market the design and that the move had been especially fortuitous because of your accident. Once I learned you'd permanently lost your memory, I thought the best I could do was get you top dollar. I've done that."

Adam sniffed. "A percentage of top dollar is not what I had in mind."

Marcus's eyes narrowed. "If you'll drop this, you can have it all."

There it was—the offer of a lifetime. He watched Marcus grab a sheet of paper and jot down an exorbitant amount.

"You can walk out of here with this amount in your pocket. Cash. We'll still handle the construction duties, but you'll get a cut of that, too."

The amount surpassed what Adam had negotiated on his own. Apparently, Steven had been right about the power of Marcus's clout. With just this initial payoff, Adam could set Renée up in a mansion, give her enough capital to hire a full staff for her business and still have plenty for himself. Yet the thought of touching money stained with his own blood left a bitter, acrid taste in his mouth. .

He chuckled, but without humor. "This isn't just about money, Marcus."

His mentor clamped his eyes shut. "I know, but that's all I have to offer. That, and my apology. I had no idea. Honestly, no idea at all."

Before Adam could break the news that the apology didn't mean squat in the great scheme of things, a lawyer flanked by two assistants burst into the room. One grabbed Marcus by the arm and dragged him aside. The other whisked Steven out of the room. Adam sank into a chair, stunned. Had he just passed up the chance of a lifetime, or had he clung to principles that ran deep in his bones?

He didn't know. He simply didn't know.

WITH HER BOTTOM LIP clamped between her teeth Sydney listened as the number of voices in the room increased. In less than five minutes, the lawyer had arrived, reportedly from his office on the fourth floor. Sydney alternated her attention between the garbled conversations on her cell phone and Bransom's call to the detective on the Tampa force. Once he disconnected, he explained that Kyle's lawyer had prepared a statement that pointed at Steven Malcolm as the man who paid him and the thugs who'd actually arranged for him to swipe the plans. Steven's so-called "associates," who'd been staking out Adam's condos and office for weeks, had yet to be named, though the criminals sure hadn't minded giving out Steven's name to Kyle. Bransom assured her that Steven Malcolm would go down, only now, with lawyers and police agencies involved, the arrest would take time.

Adam refused to leave the Malcolm offices without his original plans, so, as a show of good faith, Marcus ordered his secretary to pack them up. Adam would have his plans, but until this legal tangle was settled, he could do nothing with them. He'd refused Malcolm's offer of payment and Sydney quietly cheered.

Why take a percentage when he deserved the entire enchilada? And justice to boot?

And yet they'd come to Baltimore to close this chapter in his life. All they'd actually done is prolong the process.

The minute he emerged from the building, a long tube and a box clutched in his arms, she darted out of the car and scrambled across traffic in her high heels.

"Kind of hard to fling myself into your arms and kiss you triumphantly when you have your arms full," she said, panting in between her words. Damn, someone really needed to invent a truly sexy running shoe.

"Sorry."

He continued marching down the street, stopping at the intersection. He nodded at the dark sedan still parked across the street, but by the time Sydney turned, Detective Bransom had revved the engine and pulled into traffic, making a left at the light, heading, undoubtedly, to Flanagan's for that beer he'd been craving all morning.

"That's okay. Good romance clichés need busting up every so often. Where are we headed?"

She tried to slip the tube out from under his arm to lighten his load, but he tugged it away.

"I can handle it."

Sydney inhaled, whistling inward. Yikes. She sniffed the air, certain she'd caught a whiff of excessive testosterone. She opened her mouth to point out his rudeness then popped her lips shut. He'd just been *this* close to recapturing the future he'd cruelly lost and bringing the man who'd orchestrated his downfall to justice. Now he had a cardboard tube and an overflowing box to show for the five years he'd lost. Sydney imagined that if she were in his place, she'd be a little snippy, too.

In fact, not four days ago, she'd been in a vaguely similar situation. Nothing so dire, of course, but when she'd achieved her ultimate goal, she'd been lost, too. She'd also felt frustrated and angry, with no good place to channel those emotions except in a bottle of liquor, which hadn't helped at all. She realized just then that ever since she'd hunted down Adam, she hadn't once worried about her career or anguished over how she could possibly top debuting in the number one spot on the *New York Times*. Funny how falling in love with someone who'd lost more in one night than she'd earned in thirty years could put things into perspective.

Unable to help him with his heavy load, she instead used her slim Versace dress to entice a cab to the curb. She slid inside and waited for him to follow.

Instead he slammed the door shut and instructed the driver to deliver her to their hotel.

"Wait!" she commanded. She grabbed the half-open glass of the window and shouted one more time before Adam disappeared. "Where the hell do you think you're going?"

He took a steadying, give-me-patience breath before juggling his packages in his arms. "I need to walk. I'll meet you back at the hotel."

She stared at him, her eyes clashing with his, which were burning hot. Not with desire, but frustration. He needed to walk. Yeah, she could understand that. He probably needed to punch something or someone.

Hell, he needed to punch Steven Malcolm and his father squarely in the nose, but Sydney knew that the momentary satisfaction he might gain from violence wouldn't solve the bigger problem.

What was he going to do with his life? And how could she possibly fit into his plan?

"I'll be waiting," she finally answered, then directed the driver to merge into traffic.

She'd be waiting, but for how long? Sydney didn't know. She wasn't a patient woman and just as she'd said to Nicole and Venus back at Flanagan's, a true bad girl didn't change anything about herself unless she wanted to. She liked being impatient, damn it. She liked living in the now.

The question was, could Adam join the now with her or had today set him in the past so firmly, even she couldn't entice him back to her?

14

KEY CARD IN HAND, Adam hesitated at the door to the hotel suite, the tube of architectural plans he'd once considered priceless shoved unceremoniously into the box of files and paperwork, currently not worth the paper they were drawn on. He kicked the box lightly, struggling to contain the explosions of frustration and anger that he'd promised himself he'd lock away for another day, another time. On the bright side, at least he now knew with relative certainty that justice would come. Eventually. Unfortunately, nothing in his power could speed the process.

So for now, the only aspect of his life he could control was his relationship with Sydney. Half his heart told him to rush inside and lose himself in the fantasy of loving her, in the possibility of an exciting, unpredictable future highlighted by smart conversation, unfailing loyalty and great sex. She really was a unique woman—brave, giving and strong. Yet, she'd harnessed her take-charge attitude with flair, hardly protesting his need to work the final operation of his plan on his own. If she'd considered his intentions foolish, she hadn't uttered a single word of discouragement. She'd buoyed him with her humor, strengthened him with her irreverent style. With Sydney, a man could easily believe that he could take on the world and win without breaking a sweat.

Unfortunately, the other half of his heart reminded him that loving Sydney came with a price. From the moment she'd driven her red Corvette onto the dirt drive of his family hideaway, she'd made her intentions clear. Her days of one-night stands and meaningless affairs were over. She wanted commitment, love and, in her own free-spirited way, stability. How could he offer any of those? His future remained as undefined and diaphanous as the swirls of dust clouds she'd kicked up with her tires. Stability seemed like a far-off, unattainable fantasy. And commitment? So soon?

The only thing he could offer her was love, and even that seemed impossible since they'd been together for only two days. She had her memories of their friendship, if he could truly call it that, to base her feelings on. He only had the past three days. And yet she'd opened the doors of her heart and mind open so wide, he truly believed he knew the real Sydney Colburn, perhaps even a little better than she knew herself.

Love wasn't such a foreign feeling to him that he couldn't recognize the emotion once it crept into his heart. He respected her, admired her, cared about her with a depth that shocked the hell out of him, simply because of the time frame. And because he truly cared about her, he knew he had to suggest that they rein in their relationship before she got hurt.

Living in complacent ignorance since the accident, he'd let himself believe that recovering his missing plans would somehow instantly set his life on the right track. If he could also expose whoever had nearly killed him with their car, that would be icing on the cake. Well, he had the plans in his possession, Kyle Sanderson and Steven Malcolm being questioned by the police, a high-powered attorney assuring him they'd find justice one way or another. Yet a new direction for his life, free of the baggage, seemed no more attainable than a pot of gold at the end of a rainbow.

So, like it or not, he had to lay the truth out to Sydney, then let her decide if she was willing to wait while he sorted out his life. He didn't want her to walk away, but he wouldn't blame her if she did. But, damn, he'd miss her.

He swiped the plastic card and pushed open the door. The suite, darkened by drawn curtains, smelled of rich incense and cinnamon-scented candle wax. As he shoved the plans and files into the closet, then double-checked the lock on the hotel door, he smiled. Despite his dour mood, Sydney had managed to make him relax the minute he walked through the door.

He knew she was there, somewhere. Her presence in the suite surrounded him. The steam lingering in the shower stall. The panties hooked over the doorknob to the closet. The haunting essences of her scent, her soap, her shampoo. He tugged off his jacket, tie and belt, unbuttoned his shirt and kicked off his shoes. He emptied his pockets of his cell phone, change and wallet. Removed his socks. He wanted nothing more than to strip off the last of his clothing and discover Sydney as nude as he imagined her to be. He would bare himself to her, yes. But not in the way he wanted to. Most likely not in the way for which she'd set the scene.

In the bedroom, saxophone jazz played so softly, he barely heard any but the highest-pitched notes. He heard a rustle of sheets, a soft sigh. Was she sleeping? He'd been gone nearly six hours. Adam padded around the corner and found her just as he expected. His heart clamped in his chest.

Wrapped in the sheets, her hair damp and her face scrubbed clean and glowing in the candlelight, she looked like she'd climbed into bed just after a long, hot shower. She'd curled onto her side, one pillow between her legs, another rolled under her neck. Strategically or accidentally, the white cotton sheet exposed one breast, one bare, smooth leg, one half of her sweetly smooth backside. His sex stiffened and Adam closed his eyes, invigorated by a rush of desire. This was the second time he'd come to her like this—him, wide-awake and needing her; her, asleep and tempting. The repetition made the effect no less powerful, not when the memory of making love to her flooded his senses.

But the moment he took one step toward her, his brain flashed with the ugliness and anger and frustration he'd tried to tamp down before he returned to the hotel. After he'd left the office, he'd walked the block over to Flanagan's Pub where he'd met with Bransom, who'd suggested Adam immediately retain an attorney well versed in civil litigation. The detective hooked him up with the best barrister in town, then followed them downtown, where they met a representative from the prosecutor's office. Adam had spent four hours in interviews with people he honestly believed wanted to help him find justice. Still, they couldn't do much to expedite his wish. His five lost years meant little in the eyes of the law, particularly now that the entire fiasco was tangled in red tape, motions, charges and immunity deals.

So instead of shedding the rest of his clothes and crawling naked into bed with a woman who fired his every nerve ending, he reached forward and jiggled her awake with his hand on her toe.

"Sydney?"

"Hmmm?"

He jostled her again. "Sydney, wake up. We need to talk."

She murmured again, something that sounded fairly close to "Don't wanna talk." She shifted, and the sheet fell so that both breasts faced him, ripe and aroused.

"Sydney, sweetheart, you're killing me here."

Her eyes flashed open and she sat up with a huff.

"Don't give me ideas," she said with a growl. "Hello? Seduction? Wet, willing woman in your bed? Opportunity to take your mind off your troubles and make up for my six boring hours trapped in this hotel suite?"

Adam grinned, then sat on the corner of the mattress. He'd figured that was what she'd had in mind with the candles and the incense, though he had foolishly believed she'd honestly been asleep. He had been gone a long time, but he'd also called and left a message on her cell phone that he'd soon return.

"I should learn never to underestimate you," he admitted.

"Underestimate? Please," she said, pounding the pillows behind her, "the sleeping beauty is an age-old male fantasy. I shouldn't have picked something so predictable."

"You are never predictable."

"Then why am I failing horribly at seducing you?"

Adam shook his head. "Because you aren't trying very hard. Because you know we need to talk."

He insisted she put on a robe, but she refused, choosing only to draw the sheet up instead. Resigned, Adam updated her on the situation with the architectural designs, bringing her up to speed on his hiring an attorney here in Baltimore to represent his interests and possibly pursue civil charges against Steven Malcolm. He filled her in on both police investigations in Maryland and Florida. He laid down the facts in a tone of voice that sounded emotionless, even to his own ears. And yet she listened without comment, asking only logical, rational questions he should have thought to explain further in the first place.

When he was done presenting the bottom line—that he was no closer to regaining his former wealth or even the rights to his missing plans today than he had been a week ago—she crossed her arms over her breasts, hidden beneath the sheet, and pursed her lips.

"So that's where it stands?"

"In a nutshell," he confirmed.

"So what do we do next?"

"There's nothing to do. Both crimes, the theft and the attempted murder, happened in Florida. The police there need to make arrangements to interview Steven and weigh that interview against the information Kyle will supposedly verify once the prosecutor's office ensures his immunity. He did protect you by not telling

Steven you were with me that night and I believe he didn't know anything about the hit-and-run until after the fact. If he talks, I think we'll be good to go against Steven. I have my plans, but until the ownership of the design is validated, Marcus's deal with the Malaysians is on hold. For now, the blueprints are useless. In fact, I expect the police may take them as evidence."

A smile lit her eyes. "That's great," she concluded.

"Excuse me?"

She leaned forward, expectation practically glowing on her skin. "The plans are safely back in your possession, at least for the time being. It's just a matter of time before the whole mess is sorted out. You can move on now, Adam. You can make some decisions about your life."

"Move on? Decisions? Sydney, that's precisely what I can't do. What if I never get back the rights to the plans? I may have to prove they are mine. Steven claims I sold them to him. He has a contract with my signature on it, but because of the accident, I can't remember signing."

"Maybe you didn't. It's probably forged."

"Probably, but that's going to take proving, experts, depositions from Meg, my assistant, and my former attorney. I called him from the police station. He assures me I never would have participated in such a deal without seeking his advice."

She held her hands palm-up. "Well, there you go."

Adam shook his head. He wished he could see the mess in such simple terms, but he couldn't. "Even if I prove Steven lied, there's no guarantee that any company will want to buy the design. The bad publicity..."

"Oh, you're right," she said, dramatically serious. "And the sky could also fall tomorrow. No need to move on when there's a minute chance of impending doom."

"That's not funny," he snapped.

"I didn't mean to be funny."

"Then what did you mean?"

"That you've spent the last year recovering from your injuries, then living like a hermit while you licked your emotional wounds. That you've lived in a state of confused unknowns for long enough. Now you have answers. Now you're healed. It's time to move on. It's time to grab life by the collar and shake some excitement free."

She demonstrated by latching on to the front of his shirt and tugging herself up until they were nose to nose. With his shirt unbuttoned, the heat of her skin sizzled against his bare chest.

"Sounds so easy," he mumbled, enticed by the minty flavor of her breath, the mulled spice of her perfume.

She swiped a quick, hot kiss over his mouth. "Sorry, but it won't be easy. I'm done with easy. My whole life has been easy, in more ways than one. If I don't tackle the hard stuff right here, right now, I might never. I love you, Adam. I wish I could say I loved you before, but I wasn't capable then. If I was, I would never have walked away from you. Never."

Man, when this woman made a confession, she did so with gusto. He searched her eyes for false bravado, for any sign that she might not know what she was saying, but just as he suspected, he found none. Sydney didn't say anything she didn't truly mean.

"We've only been together for a couple of days," he reasoned.

The argument rang true, but still had a hollow echo. He hadn't admitted it out loud, but Adam loved Sydney right back. Just as the memories of their former affair were inconsequential to her, his lack of memories didn't matter, either. In a matter of days, they'd been through enough, had shared enough, to connect on a level as deep as their souls. What he felt now was real—but was love enough?

"Love is my business, Adam," she told him. "I've always tried to separate business from pleasure, fantasy from reality. But I can't anymore. Not when I'm with you. I love you and I want you in my life."

She dropped the sheet entirely, twined her fingers into his hair and slid a second kiss over his mouth. Her bare breasts brushed his chest, igniting a fire he had to put out before the flare blazed out of control.

He grabbed her waist and gently pushed her back, creating a few inches of space between them. "How do you want me?"

"Naked and hard would be a great place to start."

She shimmied her shoulders and Adam couldn't contain a chuckle. "I mean," he clarified, "how do you want me in your life? A lover? A friend? A husband?"

"All of the above," she answered, smirking as if the answer should have been obvious. "I want it all and I want it now."

She launched forward, but Adam caught her by the hands and stopped her midembrace. "I can't give it all,

Sydney. I know you want me to move on, and I will. But the time isn't right. I can't make any promises to you while the past still controls my future."

"Can't or won't?" she asked, incredulous.

He bit back a grin, but couldn't help thinking that he'd forever adore how she assumed without a doubt that he'd want her just as completely as she wanted him. Which, of course, he did. Still, her confidence and self-assured sexuality added a nuance to her personality that had crept straight into his heart.

"Is there a difference?" he asked.

She yanked her hands away. "Damn straight. *Won't* means a conscious refusal. Can't..." Her voice died away, then restarted once she'd found her words. "Adam, I don't want to rush things..."

"Yes, you do."

"Okay—yes, I do. I'm not a patient woman. I never have been. I want what I want, then I work until I get it."

"You haven't worked very long on me," he pointed out.

Her lips tightened into a grim, straight line. Her sparkling green eyes narrowed into slits. She didn't like being one-upped, particularly when he was right and she was wrong. He didn't deny that she'd spent the past three days moving heaven and earth to not only help him on his quest, but also to seduce him with every aspect of her being. He knew without a doubt that she'd given more of herself to him than she had to any other man in her life. He only questioned the time frame. Three days. He might have suffered severe head trauma, but he wasn't crazy enough to extend a marriage proposal to a woman he'd been with for less than a week. Especially when he knew she'd say yes.

Suddenly, a smile blossomed on her face. "Oh, wait, I get it. You want to me to work on you longer. Okay," she sidled up close and tugged aside his shirt. "I can handle that."

He grabbed her fingers and held them still. "That's not what I meant. Sydney Colburn…they call you Slow Burn, don't they?"

Her expression changed from expectant to serious. "Yeah…why?"

"'Cause I think it's about time you learn a little patience, woman. Learn to live up to your nickname in real life, not just in your novels."

He laid her back on the pillows, then tore the sheet away as he scrambled off the bed. She shot forward, but he chastised her with a clucking tongue. "Lie down, Slow Burn. And be still."

"But—"

"That means quiet, too. No speaking unless you're spoken to. Think you can handle that?"

"I can handle anything you can dish out," she assured him.

He counted on it.

"We'll see. Lie back, close your eyes. This will be the first test of your patience."

"How many tests will there be?"

"I don't know. You're already failing the quiet test."

She opened her mouth, then smacked her lips closed. That was his Sydney, a quick study.

"Eyes closed?"

He glanced around the room while waiting for her

reply, then realized she wasn't going to say a word. Good for her. When he caught sight of her panty hose draped over a chair, an idea sprung to mind. He grabbed them, found a pair of thong panties—these a nude shade—in her suitcase, and tucked them in his pocket. He wanted her to know that pleasure delayed was pleasure worth waiting for. He needed her to see that sticking with him for a long haul, even with no immediate promise of commitment, could be an exciting, thrilling adventure.

He glanced over his shoulder as he pawed through the dresses she'd hung in her closet. "You look a little tense, Sydney."

She was lying on her back, her hands folded over her abdomen, her legs crossed at the ankles.

"Why don't you spread your legs a little?" He found the green dress she'd worn earlier and tugged it off the hanger. "Let me see you. All of you."

A tiny smile played over her lips, then she uncrossed her ankles and slowly inched her feet apart. From the shadows of her curls, he saw the sweet pink flesh of her sex. His mouth watered for a taste, his nostrils flared in search of her scent.

But he'd need to show a little patience, as well. He continued to the closet.

"Now your hands. What to do with your hands?"

She unhooked her fingers, presumably to answer his question with action, but he stopped her with a deep-throated cough. "Oh, no. I'm in charge tonight, Sydney."

Her eyes sprung open and she ignored his edict

about speaking. "I thought you were only interested in teaching me patience?"

"A little patience, a little submission." He waggled his eyebrows. "Work with me."

"What if you ask me to do something I don't want to do? As you've so painfully pointed out, you've only known me for three days. Maybe I'm not so daring, deep down. Maybe it's all been an act."

A raw sound accompanied her words, causing Adam to abandon his plan to dress her, then undress her. For now. He'd assumed too much, believing she needed action over words since that's what she'd told him on the golf course. But perhaps she needed both. Of course she did. She was a woman. In essence, just like any other.

And yet like none he'd ever met.

Clutching the silky material of her dress in his hands, he stalked to the edge of the bed and watched her eyes mist with emotions, one of which was anger.

"Tell me what you want, Sydney."

"Why? So you can make me wait for it? Teach me some lesson? I'm a big girl, Adam."

"What does that mean? That you know everything?"

"I know I love you."

"And I know I love you right back."

She pulled her knees to her chest, wrapping her arms around them, surprise evident in her face. "You do?"

He slid next to her and carefully laid the dress across the bedspread. "I honestly believe I do. In three days, I've fallen in love with you."

"Then why are we still playing games?" She

smoothed her hand down his arm. "Make love to me, Adam."

"And then what?"

She straightened her spine, her eyes wide. "I don't know. We make love again? We go home to Florida. We play more games, make up our own rules."

"Our rules or your rules? You want a husband. I'm not ready, but I want you. Most women would consider that chasm too deep to cross."

"I'm not most women."

"No, you're not," he answered, grinning like a fool. She eyed him sideways and, from her glance, he knew she was beginning to understand. Or at least she was willing to try.

"You like that green dress?"

He blew out a low-pitched whistle. "Thinking about that green dress has kept me sane all day. I thought I'd have you put it on, then I'd enjoy the pleasure of removing it."

She pursed her lips and nodded. "This is a lesson in patience, huh?"

"Patience, teasing. Temptation."

She swiped the panty hose and thong from his pocket. "Well, you know what Mae West said about temptation, don't you?"

She slid off the bed, grabbed the chair by the window and moved it closer to the table where she'd set a half-dozen candles glimmering with flickers of fire. She placed the thong underwear over the top of the chair and did the same with her dress.

Adam stole her place on the bed, propped himself

against pillows scented by her, and prepared to watch and direct a delicious private show.

"What did Mae say?" he asked.

"Something along the lines of 'I generally avoid temptation—unless I can't resist it.'"

She flicked out the lacy-topped thigh-high hose, then eased into the chair with one leg extended long and lean over the arm, the other tilted out so that as she donned the sheer, black stockings, he'd be able to watch the play of light over her glistening intimate flesh.

"And you can't resist trying things my way for a while?" he asked, hopeful.

She answered with the most wicked, most alluring, bad-girl grin he'd ever seen. She rolled the material into a soft ball, then stretched her toes inside. "I can't resist you, Adam Brody. So we'll give this patience thing a shot. Now, sit back and watch Slow Burn Colburn show you how it's done."

Epilogue

IT'S ABOUT DAMN TIME.

Try as she might over the last eight months, Sydney Colburn decided that her newly expanded capacity for patience had a limit. From that night back in Baltimore when Adam had hijacked the reins of their lovemaking and forced her to experience a slow tease, Sydney knew her ability to forgo instant gratification wouldn't last. That she'd managed over two hundred and forty days—two hundred and forty-three to be exact—shocked the hell out of her.

And yet the memory of dressing for Adam, then allowing him to undress her, giving him the power to direct each and every experiment in pleasure, still ignited a hot thrill deep in her belly, along with a quick throb even lower. True love had indeed rocked her into the world of unknown possibilities, even with regards to sex. And she'd loved each and every minute.

Still, she'd had enough of the waiting.

Staring out across the open deck of what she hoped would become their third-story bedroom, currently no more than four-by-four planks and scaffolding with plenty of space for the bank of floor-to-ceiling windows, Sydney watched the vast Florida wilderness fade with the coming sunset. Many times, Sydney had used her favorite time of day in her books as symbolism for endings. But this evening, the spectrum of pinks and purples meant a new beginning—freedom from her past and Adam's, and the fresh start they'd made together.

Only a week ago, Steven Malcolm had started serving his jail sentence for his role in Adam's accident. Steven and Kyle had both cooperated with the police investigations, but while the former courier had received only probation for his part in the crimes, Steven had to serve time, despite his plea bargain. The only lack of justice came for the hired guns who'd run Adam down with their car. Reportedly, they'd fled the country. But since Steven had set the crimes in motion with his jealousy, both Sydney and Adam were satisfied that he would pay, not only with ten to fifteen years of his life, but with his once-sterling reputation.

In his negotiated settlement with Marcus Malcolm, Adam had reclaimed several designs he'd created while at the firm, as well as the architectural plans to the innovative office center that had finally made him a very wealthy man. But the plans for this house—one of his very first projects—had been even more special. To both of them. Both a nod to Adam's lost past and a monument to his bright future.

The moment Sydney had seen the blueprints, she'd fallen in love—with the house. She'd already loved the man for approximately two hundred and forty-*six* days—soon after she'd laid eyes on him in worn blue jeans and a tool belt. Likely, even before.

And thanks to her suggestion that he build the place on the off chance that this infernal waiting game might end in a wedding, she'd been able to see him dressed in his work clothes a whole lot lately. His visits to the con-

struction site had started as supervisory, but, before
long, he'd torn off his shirt and joined the paid labor.
Sydney had rented a small air-conditioned trailer so
she could watch as she worked on her new book. And
with her so close by, they made love whenever the
mood struck them, ate picnic lunches under century-
old trees, shared thoughts and dreams of the future.

The future! It had taken Adam long enough to embrace the concept, but now Sydney was ready to turn
tomorrow into today.

In addition to the bulk of the profit from the final
deal with the Malaysians, Adam received enough in financial compensation to build this dream home on a
lush parcel of land just inland from the Gulf of Mexico.
In the distance, she could hear the rumble and rattle of
Adam's old truck, winding through the thick pines and
palms that lined the unpaved driveway. A mile from
the nearest shell-covered road and surrounded by pro-
tected wetlands, they'd found a bucolic, private hideaway.

She'd keep her condo, too, of course. No way could
she remain this far from Nieman Marcus without suffering withdrawal. But for the bulk of their week, while
he built houses, she'd work in the quiet serenity of the
Florida wilderness, her love for Adam having reinvig-
orated her love for writing. She appreciated the bestseller lists now only because they meant she reached
more and more readers every day with her stories of
love and redemption. Her current work in progress—
the steamy tale of a man suffering from amnesia after
battling Robert the Bruce, and the woman seeking to
seduce his memory back—was fairly flying from her

fingertips onto the screen of her computer. She'd probably turn the completed manuscript in to her editor early, leaving her plenty of time for a wedding and honeymoon.

Now she just needed the groom.

When she heard Adam's truck hit gravel, she knew he'd be at the unfinished house in seconds. She slipped behind one of the completed interior walls, glancing around one last time to make sure everything was in place. She peered out, and certain Adam had come alone, she scurried over to the bed she'd had delivered that morning. She'd paid through the nose to have her request fulfilled on a Sunday when she'd be sure no construction workers would be around, but the price would be worth it. She arranged herself on the bed for maximum seduction and did the waiting thing, relying on the notes she'd placed strategically around the unfinished house to lure Adam upstairs.

"Sydney?"

His voice spawned an intense wave of desire over her skin, then through her body. The night would be cool, but heat still shot through the sunset hour like a stream of warm water in the gulf. She wore nothing but three red bows—one tied over her breasts and one twined lower to form a makeshift bikini bottom, and one dangling around her neck, weighted by a velvet pouch and the rings she'd purchased from a special jeweler she'd discovered on a weeklong research trip to New Orleans.

The thought of placing that ring on Adam made her bite her lip, keeping her from answering his calls. *Fol-*

low the notes, she repeated silently, willing herself to complete this one last act of patient expectation.

His footfalls, increasingly urgent, matched the un-bridled beat of her heart. This was it. The breaking point. The moment of no return. She lay back into the fluffy new pillows she'd placed all over the bed, swathed in silk, and silently hoped that her patience and Adam's resolve to wait before they committed their relationship had run out at the same time.

"Sydney?"

He filled the doorway with his broad shoulders, trim waist and long, lean legs. Shadows of the oncoming night blocked his expression, but by the way he clutched the doorjamb, she knew she'd surprised him. Good. She was afraid they'd gotten to know each other so well over the last eight months that she'd lost the ability to shock the hell out of him.

"Now there's a present I can't wait to unwrap," he said with a libidinous growl.

She held up a hand, stopping him midway across the large room. "Patience, Adam."

When he ripped off his shirt and tore away the laces on his boots, she couldn't contain a giggle. Many times over the past eight months, she'd been the one to tease him, to deny him, to make him work for the luxury of making love with her. But mainly, he'd been the one to make her wait, denying her the fast and furious pace; the spontaneous, exciting quickies she so enjoyed. Not that they hadn't slipped every so often, but she de-cided today they'd remain true to their agreement to take things slowly, savor the moment.

If for no other reason than to torture him.

In seconds, he was naked, standing proud and hard at the edge of the bed. "You've been gone a whole week, Syd. You disappear on a trip to New Orleans without a word—although I'm definitely not complaining about the nightly phone sex. But then you leave a message on my cell phone that you're back in town and waiting for me, and you expect me to be patient?"

She laughed, loving the frantic, barely contained lust in his voice.

"Yes. I'll be worth the wait, I promise. But first I have a gift for you."

He shoved his hands onto his lean, naked hips. "Looks like you have three gifts for me. Do I get to chose which one I open first?"

A thrill shot through her and she wondered which bow he'd free first, if she allowed him the pick. Her breasts? Her nipples tightened into electrified pearls, just remembering all the time he'd spent learning precisely how to pleasure her with his fingers, mouth and teeth. More than once, he'd tortured her for what seemed like hours on end, using his sensual talents only on her breasts, no matter how she bucked and begged for deeper satisfaction. Suddenly, the bow she'd twined around her sex, a thick red swath of silk and satin, seemed to tighten, constrain. The promise of feeling him buried deep inside her, his hardness to her soft heat, nearly made her stray from her original plan.

"No. See the pouch around my neck?" She curled her arms beneath her head, well aware how the movement made her breasts jut out. "That's the first one."

He made a gruff noise something along the lines of a

frustrated sigh, but did as she instructed and removed the pouch from around her neck. Tearing the strings open, he shook the gold contents out onto his palm.

"What the heck is this?"

She laughed. She figured he wouldn't know. She hadn't known either, until the jewelry's designer had explained.

"The large loop goes around your cock. The small ring attaches to your ear. You're supposed to wear it beneath your clothes whenever you want me to...yank your chain, so to speak."

His eyebrow darted up. "Where the hell did you find this contraption?"

Sydney shook her head, not the least surprised or daunted by Adam's reaction. She didn't expect him to accept such a far-out sex aid without skepticism, even one made out of fourteen-carat gold and encrusted with tiny diamonds.

"At a gallery in New Orleans. They specialize in erotic art and jewelry."

He pinched the small loop between his fingers and let the large one drop. When he held the earring beside his ear, the bottom hoop only barely reached his waist. "Looks like this was designed for a shorter man."

"It's adjustable. But it's a ring of sorts, right? I'm giving you a ring, Adam."

A moment passed before the significance of what she'd said solidified in his mind. In an instant, he was laughing so hard, she thought he might break something. He had to sit on the bed and brace his hands on his knees to catch his breath.

She sat up, not sure whether or not to be annoyed.

When he wiped a tear from the corner of his eye and then grabbed her by both bows and pulled her into his arms, she forgot to care.

"Only you would use a cock ring to ask a man to marry you."

She shrugged. "I'm bad to the bone, what can I say?"

He grabbed the jeans he'd discarded on the corner of the bed and dragged them over. "Now you can say what you think of the gift I brought you."

He dug into the pocket and pulled out a small jewelry box. She'd known that she and Adam often followed the same wavelength, but she could barely allow herself to hope that he'd finally come to the same conclusion she had months ago.

Forgetting her bows, Sydney tore open the tiny box to find a bright platinum band of baguette diamonds, centered by a bright green emerald.

She looked up at him, speechless. His warm, light brown eyes brimmed with undeniable love.

"Marry me, Sydney. I may take a more traditional path sometimes, but my life won't be complete without you."

Swallowing, Sydney opened her mouth to say yes, but she didn't have the breath to push the single word over her lips. When he twisted so that she sat on the bed and he knelt at her feet, she knew she was lost. Tears streamed down her face as he cupped her hands in his.

"Are you at a loss for words? Should I call someone?"

His crack broke through the overwhelmingly wave of emotion. "You can call whomever you like. No one will believe that I was speechless anyway. Adam, this is gorgeous."

"You're gorgeous. And unpredictable and exciting and brazen as hell. I couldn't love you any more than I do right now. Please, Sydney Colburn. Be my wife."

She closed her eyes and forced the thick lump of emotion down her throat. Unable to resist, she asked, "Do you promise to wear my gift whenever I ask you to?"

He rolled his eyes. "I'm already your love slave, Sydney. If you promise to never allow my life to be forgettable, I promise to make every fantasy of yours come true."

"Yes, Adam, yes. I'll marry you."

The minute he pushed her back onto the bed and began unwrapping the rest of her ribbons, Sydney knew she'd not only learned the real-life advantages of a true slow burn, but she'd found a man who would twist her bad girl ways into something wonderful—now and for always.

* * * * *

Wait! The fun isn't over yet!
There is still one more bad girl
waiting to send some guy's life into a tailspin.
Watch for

RED-HOT & RECKLESS

by Tori Carrington, available next month.
The BAD GIRLS CLUB—
membership has its privileges!

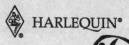

HARLEQUIN® Duets™

TWO ROMANTIC COMEDIES IN ONE FUN VOLUME!

Don't miss double the laughs in

Once Smitten
and
Twice Shy

From acclaimed Duets author
Darlene Gardner

Once Smitten—that's Zoe O'Neill and Jack Carter, all right! It's a case of "the one who got away" and Zoe's out to make amends!

In *Twice Shy,* Zoe's two best friends, Amy Donatelli and Matt Burke, are alone together for the first time and each realizes they're "the one who never left!"

Any way you slice it, these two tales serve up a big dish of romance, with lots of humor on the side!

Volume #101
Coming in June 2003

Available at your favorite retail outlet.

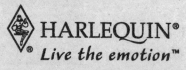

HARLEQUIN®
Live the emotion™

Visit us at www.eHarlequin.com

HDDD99DG

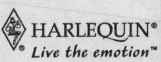

A "Mother of the Year" contest brings
overwhelming response as thousands of women
vie for the luxurious grand prize....

Kate Hoffmann

Jacqueline Diamond

Jill Shalvis

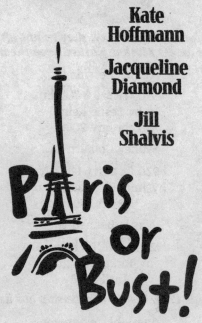

Paris or Bust!

A hilarious and romantic trio of new stories!

With a trip to Paris at stake, these women are
determined to win! But the laughs are many as three of
them discover that being finalists isn't the most
excitement they'll ever have.... Falling in love is!

Available in April 2003.

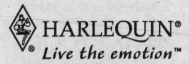

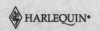
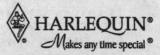

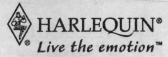